PEACEMAKER LAW

PEACEMAKER
LAW

•

CLIFFORD BLAIR

AVALON BOOKS
THOMAS BOUREGY AND COMPANY, INC.
401 LAFAYETTE STREET
NEW YORK, NEW YORK 10003

PRINTED IN THE UNITED STATES OF AMERICA
ON ACID-FREE PAPER
BY HADDON CRAFTSMEN, SCRANTON, PENNSYLVANIA

IN MEMORIAM

Dr. Clifford Jennings Blair:
Beloved father, husband,
and physician.
You are sorely missed.

Chapter One

"I think," Prudence McKay said, "that I need to retain your services."

James Stark leaned back from the dinner table and gave her a questioning look. He couldn't erase the wry smile that moved his lips. "You mean this isn't a social occasion?" he inquired.

Prudence had the grace to color prettily.

Looking past her dark-haired head, Stark, as he had planned by long-standing habit, had a clear view of the rest of the elegant restaurant with its chattering diners and busy waiters. The Golden Apple was the height of dining fashion in Guthrie. Here the cosmopolitan elite of the Victorian capital of Oklahoma Territory met and mingled and gossiped and conducted business over the evening meal.

Stark had already picked out a judge, several politicians, and some local businessmen, as well as cattlemen, Eastern speculators, railroad executives, a land baron or two, and other high-dollar grifters. In attendance upon them were their womenfolk—ladies and otherwise—all decked out in their nicest evening finery. There was a constant flow to and from the elaborate gambling hall in the next room.

Stark figured a top gun hand and troubleshooter like

himself fit in with this motley pack as well as anybody else present.

He glanced back at his dinner companion. To his mind, Prudence McKay, attorney and counselor-at-law, put all the other womenfolk here to shame. She had her dark brown hair done up in curls with a yellow ribbon, and wore a matching frilled dress with a modest neckline. Always easy on the eyes, even when attired for a court appearance, tonight she was an enchanting vision. Stark was, he decided, much more interested in watching her fetching reaction to his question, and in getting an answer to it, than he was in eyeballing the rest of the restaurant's patrons.

"Of course I enjoy your company, James," she told him demurely. "But I do have need of you as an expert witness."

Stark blinked. He had wondered what was behind her dinner invite and the fine steak she'd fed him, but he hadn't expected this. For the most part, she tended to disapprove of his profession.

"Expert on what?" he asked bluntly.

"Why, on guns, naturally. Everyone knows your reputation as a marksman and a . . . a . . ."

"Gunfighter?" he supplied laconically.

Her full red lips thinned slightly. Was a time she had applied that term to him herself in not too complimentary a fashion. "I was about to say peacemaker," she said levelly.

James Stark: Peacemaker for Hire. That was what it said on his card, and it was the name under which he did business. "Tell me about your case and what you need from me," he suggested.

"My client is accused of shooting a man at long range, using his pistol."

Gunplay was common, and toting a gun nothing unusual in Oklahoma Territory, parts of which were still sanctuaries for outlaws, bandits, and wanted men. Going unarmed was more the exception than the rule outside of Guthrie's reasonably civilized limits.

Though he wasn't packing his custom bowie knife or his ten-gauge Winchester lever-action, Stark himself wasn't unarmed this night. His Colt .45 single-action Army revolver—the Peacemaker from which he'd taken his nickname—rode comfortably in its holster beneath the tail of his corduroy coat. The little Marlin .38 double-action revolver in the concealed holster at the small of his back would've made sitting uncomfortable if he hadn't grown so accustomed to its presence. Now its absence would've prodded him with unease. A man with his rep would be a fool not to pack a shooting iron, even in the Golden Apple.

"What kind of gun was your client using?"

"A Remington 1875 single-action Army revolver," Prudence answered promptly.

Stark wasn't surprised at her knowledge. No fan of firearms was Prudence, he knew; still, she would've made herself familiar with every pertinent fact of her client's case.

She was watching him closely for his reaction. "How long of a shot?" he probed further.

"Almost a hundred fifty yards. I measured it off myself."

Stark snorted.

"Well?" Prudence demanded. "Could it be done?"

"A hundred fifty yards? With an 1875 Remington Army? Not likely."

Prudence's smile was triumphant. "What about you? Could you do it?"

"Maybe if I knew the gun, and got real lucky," Stark conceded. "But I wouldn't bet the farm on it."

Her enthusiasm was dampened only a little by his qualifier. "But you'd be willing to testify that only a trained marksman would have the slightest chance of making a shot like that?" She pressed him as if he was a hostile witness on the stand.

The daughter of a Kansas judge, Prudence McKay had studied law back East, and here in the Territory had rapidly earned a worthy reputation in the courtroom. She had successfully represented Stark himself on one occasion.

"Well?" she demanded, then broke off as she caught the direction of Stark's gaze. Turning her head, she looked over her shoulder at the two men approaching the table.

Stark had been idly noting them as they made the rounds of the tables. He and Prudence seemed to be next in their path. The man in the lead was big, with the beginnings of softness that hung on a frame that had once been hard and fit. The hardness still showed in the dark cool eyes set in his well-hewn features. His face had not yet given way to the fleshiness that had begun to claim the rest of him. In a tailored suit, complete with diamond stickpin and gold watch chain, he cut an impressive figure. Stark couldn't see a gun, but the big hombre moved like he was armed. Likely a hideout gun somewhere on him, Stark mused. And, likely, he knew how to use it.

Behind him, gliding catlike in his wake, was a tall, thin Chinese in a plain oversize suit much less expensive than that of his companion. Automatically Stark felt tension flow through him. Over a long and checkered career he had seen only a few men move with the same fluid ease as the Oriental. One of them had been the Frenchman Joseph Charlemont, who had taught Stark the finer points of *savate,* and who was one of the greatest masters of that brutal art of French foot fighting.

The Oriental's lean face was about as expressive as a closed door. He wore heavy clodhopper shoes and didn't look to have a gun.

"Mr. Burke!" Prudence spoke up. "What a pleasant surprise!" Stark noted the back of her pale neck taking on a faint rosy hue.

"It's Randall, please. I thought we had that settled." Beaming, the big man came to a halt beside their table, taking Prudence's hand in both of his. His hands looked as hard as his eyes. The Chinese hovered watchfully in the background.

Stark inched his chair back.

"No, please don't get up." Even preoccupied with Prudence, Randall Burke had noted the movement.

Stark wasn't being polite. He wanted to be able to move fast if it was called for. Something about the pair rubbed his fur the wrong way. "Friend of yours?" he drawled to Prudence.

She squared her slender shoulders almost defiantly. "Yes," she asserted. "A friend and a client."

"You're James Stark, the Peacemaker," Burke said, slipping smoothly into the conversation. "I know of you, but I've never had the pleasure of meeting you." His dark eyes seemed to weigh Stark coolly. "Pinkerton-trained; one-time lawman and bounty hunter; hiring out now as troubleshooter, range detective, bodyguard, and confidential investigator."

"You looking to hire me?"

Burke laughed. "Not today." He gestured at the silent Oriental lurking at his back. "Chin here takes care of any trouble that comes down the pike in my direction."

Stark flicked his eyes at the bodyguard as he heard Prudence say, "Randall owns the Golden Apple."

"And I'm pleased to have two such prominent citizens of Guthrie in my establishment. I owe a lot to Prudence here."

"Is that fact?" Stark shifted his gaze back to Burke.

"It sure is." Burke dropped a hand as if to brush it across Prudence's shoulder in a casual caress. Prudence avoided it with a graceful shift that looked inadvertent. Burke didn't appear to notice as he kept talking. "She helped me draw up the papers when I opened this place. She's a mighty fine lawyer."

That took care of the client part, Stark tallied. He was still wondering about the friend part of Prudence's relationship with this hombre. "You've got a nice place here," he commented without inflection.

"Well, feel welcome anytime." Burke gave him a slick smile.

Strains of music drifted across the room. Stark saw that a handful of musicians had taken the small stage next to the dance floor. A few couples were already drifting in that direction.

''Why, there's the ensemble,'' Burke said, as though surprised by their presence. ''Prudence, would you be so kind as to give me the honor of the first dance?''

Prudence's head tipped back a fraction. ''Of course,'' she said, rising, ''so long as it's a quick one.'' If there was a message in the brief glance she gave Stark, he couldn't read it.

Graciously Burke offered his arm. She extended her hand so that the tips of her fingers were just barely brushing the fabric of his fancy suit.

''No objections, I trust, Mr. Stark?'' Burke inquired blandly.

''Don't step on any toes.''

Burke escorted her away, leaving Stark with the sudden sour hunch that the man had plotted all along to be at this table when the band that he employed struck up the first waltz so that he could claim Prudence as his partner. They made a fine-looking couple too, he had to admit.

Chin drifted casually in their wake. With hooded eyes Stark watched the Chinaman until he took up an out-of-the-way post near the stage. From there he commanded a wide view of the dance floor. He stood, arms crossed, face still like a door.

Prudence and Burke were whirling gracefully about amid the other couples. The restaurant owner moved with surprising lightness. Prudence held herself a decorous distance from him. As he glimpsed her face, Stark saw only polite attention on her features.

He had no brand on Prudence, he reflected sullenly. No man did. But the fellow who did place one on her would have his corral full of trouble mighty fast. Prudence was too headstrong, too independent, for most men. Certainly for the Peacemaker.

But headstrong filly or not, Randall Burke's time with her had just about run out.

Stark pushed his chair back from the table and strode toward the dance floor. He sensed the quickening gaze of the bodyguard, Chin, on him as he moved out among the dancers. The men swung their partners from his path. Neither Prudence nor Burke seemed aware of his coming.

"No objections to me cutting in, I trust?" He slipped an arm between the two of them and moved deftly to take Burke's place as the big man shifted back automatically.

Prudence's eyes sparkled. She followed his lead as though his move had been rehearsed, and, in the space of a breath, they had left Burke standing alone in the center of the swirling couples. Stark had a fleeting look of the man's handsome, reddening face.

Prudence fit nicely into his arms, he found. The musicians were skilled, and the music seemed to lift and move them into the rhythm of the dance. Prudence's lovely face filled his vision. Her tantalizing nearness, her fingers entwined with his, the smooth fabric of her dress beneath his palm, touched Stark with a heady exhilaration so that he almost forgot his surroundings.

Somewhat shaken at his own involvement, he wheeled them clear of the dance floor as the waltz ended. Prudence too seemed a bit unsteady as they regained their table.

Stark seated her, then moved to his own chair, catching the polite little bow Burke offered her from across the room. Prudence smiled slightly and dipped her head in response.

"Nice clientele you have," Stark commented as he took his seat.

Prudence bristled like a goaded bobcat. "He's an upstanding businessman and a perfect gentleman!"

"I wouldn't know about the first, but as to the second, he's hardcase to the bone under that high-dollar suit and fancy talk."

"Something like you?" she retorted.

"Not like me." Stark's tone was flat. "I don't need a hired killer to bail me out of a fracas."

"Chin's a servant," Prudence protested.

"He's a trained killer. Probably better with his bare hands than any other weapon, but I wouldn't rank him as a tenderfoot in any kind of a scrap."

Prudence clamped her lips together as if to hold back a response. She turned her gaze to the dance floor for a long moment. Stark thought it lingered briefly on Chin. Then Prudence's eyes returned to him. "I didn't ask you here to argue, or to discuss Randall Burke. I asked you here to talk about a client, and see if you'd be willing to help me. Will you testify for my client or not?"

Stark reined himself in. One of these days he'd manage to be around Prudence more than a handful of minutes without tangling with her, he told himself ruefully. "I'll do what I can," he answered her aloud.

"That's wonderful." Her relieved smile flashed.

Burke and Chin disappeared into the gambling hall. Stark noted a wiry young wrangler ambling in their wake.

He nodded at the dance floor. "Care for another turn?" he asked Prudence.

"I'd love it."

She was breathless and radiant when they returned to the table. Stark was having a little trouble drawing air himself.

"I really must be getting home," Prudence said with evident reluctance. "I've got hearings tomorrow."

Outside, she dismissed his suggestion of taking one of the hired carriages lined up at the curb. "Let's walk," she suggested instead. "It's nice out."

The early fall air was cool, but it felt good to Stark after the warmth of the restaurant. Prudence let him drape her shawl over her shoulders, then took the arm he offered. Together they strolled along the cobblestones of Harrison Street beneath the flickering illumination of the gas streetlamps. The plush Palace Hotel, where Prudence lived, wasn't far, and Stark found himself slowing his step a little.

They passed the imposing facade of the three-story Reaves Brothers Casino, which, Stark calculated, was Burke's biggest competitor for the capital's uptown gaming customers. Opposite the casino was the rowdy Blue Bell Saloon. Stark eyed it warily as they passed on the far side of the street. Then he stiffened.

"What's wrong?" Prudence must've felt his tension.

"A little trouble over yonder," Stark said without looking around. Her gasp told him that she had spotted it. Her hand dropped from his arm.

In the dim alley beside the saloon, shadow forms bobbed and moved. Stark saw the distinctive flailing motions of punches being thrown. He heard the sound of impacts and the grunts of pain they elicited. A wiry figure cringed beneath the assault of a trio of attackers. Three to one. Bad odds for any man.

"Oh, can't you stop them?" Prudence cried.

"I reckon," Stark answered and cut across the street toward the alley.

Chapter Two

The three rowdies—maybe patrons of the Blue Bell Saloon—had their victim hemmed against the wall, battering at him with fists and boots. Stark approached warily; then his stride lengthened as he drew nearer. He was running for the last four steps he took. Six feet distant, he hurled himself into the air, twisting his body sideward, right leg cocked under him. His booted left foot, with all the force of his hurtling weight behind it, drove outward to slam full against the head of the biggest hardcase, like the kick of a spooked bronc. A tattered Stetson sailed off into the darkness of the alley, and the burly yahoo crashed against his cronies.

One of them almost went down beneath the limp form. But the other twisted clear with agile speed. His hand moved like the strike of a rattler to whip a fighting blade clear of its sheath. Stark had a glimpse of the startled, vaguely familiar face of the victim where he slumped against the wall. Then the knife came swiping around at Stark's gut.

Stark bent his arm to guard his middle, rocked back and thrust the hard sole of his boot full into the knifer's chest. It stopped him cold in his tracks, gasping for air. Stark slashed at the knife wrist with his left, sent the blade spinning away after the Stetson. He crossed a right to the rowdy's hanging jaw, followed it with a left straight from his shoulder. His scarred knuckles slammed square between the ranny's eyes. That punch might've dropped him, but before he could fall, Stark set his feet and ripped an uppercut under the whiskered chin. The lift of his shoulder behind the blow sent the hardcase ambling backward as if all his joints had come unhinged. He sagged.

''Draw, you sorry son!'' a shrill voice cried.

The third hombre had shoved his bigger pard aside and squared off like a gunfighter, fingers poised over the butt of his pistol. Stark knew his breed at a glance. He'd seen gun-hungry punks like this all across the territory. Looking to gain a rep with a six-shooter, most of them gained nothing but a bed of dirt. He'd been forced to put more than one of them there himself.

The other two rowdies were out of action for the moment—maybe longer. The victim was hunched at the edge of Stark's vision. He hoped Prudence had stayed clear. He didn't like the notion of bullets flying with her hereabouts.

''Pull in your horns, kid,'' Stark advised coldly. ''The name is Stark; James Stark.''

A strangled grunt came from the husky one, now on his knees. ''That's the Peacemaker, Stace!'' he gasped hoarsely. ''Let it ride!''

''Are you loco?'' Stace exclaimed. ''This is my big chance! Think what it'd mean to be the man who downed the Peacemaker!''

''Won't mean anything if you're dead,'' Stark told him. ''I'm warning you; back off.'' The image of Prudence flickered briefly in his mind. She rued gunwork and the role it played in his life.

"I'll back off!" the rowdy spat. "Like this!" His clawed hand grasped his pistol and jerked it upward.

The downward sweep of Stark's own hand brushed his coattail aside, and the familiar heft of the .45 seemed to spring to his grip. He brought it out and level and cocked with a single snapping flick of his wrist.

His gun half-drawn, staring at death, the hardcase froze rigid as a fence post. Stark stilled the final pressure of his finger. It was hard not to pump lead into an hombre hankering to kill him, but maybe there was no need for this gun-hungry kid to die.

And, could be, he wouldn't be so hungry anymore.

"Pull that hogleg the rest of the way, then drop it," Stark ordered. As the kid complied, Stark darted his eyes to the other two yahoos. Neither of them was offering any more fight.

"We didn't mean no harm, Mr. Stark," the one on his knees babbled like some supplicant seeking forgiveness.

Behind the speaker, the knifer Stark had hammered with his fists sat up unsteadily. "You two shuck your guns," Stark told them.

He was conscious of the victim straightening from where he had been hunched against the wall. He looked ready to continue the fight, but smart enough not to get in the way of Stark's gun.

"Are you all right, Jim?" Prudence asked in a concerned tone. She had approached to the mouth of the alley.

"I'm fine." Stark didn't want to take his attention off the rowdies. "Check on him." He tilted his head sideward toward the victim.

"I ain't hurt none," the fellow said with a growl. "These varmints got lucky is all. Didn't like me snooping around, I reckon."

"Three-to-one odds don't need luck," Stark told him out of the corner of his mouth. He wagged his gun at the trio of rowdies. "You boys scatter. Leave your irons here. Each of you hightail it in a different direction. You cause this gent any more trouble, you'll answer to me. Savvy?"

He got an assortment of disgruntled nods.

"Vamoose!"

They took off, following orders. Stark listened to the fading sounds of their boots on the cobblestones, then thumbed down the hammer on the Colt. Holstering it, he turned his full attention for the first time on the man he'd rescued.

He saw a youngish bronc buster, disheveled from the beating he'd taken, but otherwise in good enough shape. It took a puzzled moment for Stark to recognize the hombre he'd seen in The Golden Apple following Burke and his Chinese henchman.

"You're the Peacemaker?" the stranger demanded before Stark could speak.

"Yep."

"Ronald Hall." He stuck out an eager hand. "Most folks just call me Ronnie. I'm mighty obliged, Mr. Stark!"

"Glad to help." Stark gripped the work-hardened palm. "This here's Miss McKay."

"A pleasure, ma'am," Ronnie said in a rush, hesitating only a pair of seconds over her fetching looks. Plainly he had more on his mind than polite introductions. "Really something, running into you this way, Mr. Stark," he went on hurriedly.

"That a fact?" Stark said.

"Yessir. Happens you're the man we came down here to see."

Stark stepped back so the shorter man could come a little farther into the light. Self-consciously Ronnie slapped dust from his well-worn range clothes and bent to retrieve his Stetson, which he'd lost during the fracas. He moved with the lazy economy of a man used to working with horses. Stark saw that he wore a gun, but it was too high, and too far back on his hip, to be brought into play with any kind of real speed. It said something good about his character that he'd been willing to tangle bareknuckle with three bigger men rather than turn a brawl into a shooting scrap.

Ronnie's eyes had been drawn to Prudence a second time, and he was gazing at her almost raptly, as if really seeing her at last.

"You say you want to talk business with me?" Stark prodded him gruffly.

"Huh? Oh, yeah, we do."

"Who's we?"

"The two fellows that came down here with me from Indian Territory. Andrew Blaine spoke real highly of you to us."

"Be at my office, eight o'clock tomorrow morning. I'll talk to you then."

"Yessir. You can bet we'll be there." With one last

moon-struck look at Prudence he slipped past them out of the alley.

Stark watched him go until he was sure the trio of hardcases hadn't regrouped to lie in wait for him. He became aware of Prudence gazing up at him.

"I'm glad you weren't hurt," she told him softly, and he felt the touch of her fingers on his arm. "For a moment, when you drew your gun, I thought you were going to—"

"So did I," Stark cut her off dryly.

He took his leave of her in her hotel lobby, the sensation of her touch still lingering as he ankled back to the hostelry where he made his residence. He kept an eye peeled, but thankfully there was still no sign of the ambitious Stace or his pards. Before dropping off to sleep he remembered he'd neglected to get any further details about Prudence's client to whose cause he'd committed himself.

After breakfast in the hotel dining room, he legged it to his office, wondering if Ronnie and his compatriots would keep their appointment. The growth of his reputation as a troubleshooter, and the resulting business and income, had made it needful for him to hire a combination bookkeeper and office manager to handle his affairs, particularly during his frequent journeys elsewhere in the territory. When he was present in Guthrie, like now, he gave her the mornings off and opened the office himself.

He drcw up slightly as he saw the three men awaiting him at his office door. Then, recognizing the wiry Ronnie, he continued his approach. He greeted them as he produced the key to the door.

He ushered them through the empty reception area and into his office. They paused a moment, surveying the high-ceiling room.

Stark's big oak desk was against a side wall, out of the line of sight of the windows. The rusted skeleton of an old revolver and a long-bladed Arkansas toothpick acted as paperweights on the orderly stacks of documents and folders on its battered surface. An ornate, framed certificate from his days as a Pinkerton was mounted on the wall behind his chair. Beside it hung a lawman's silver star framed on a bed of dark velvet. Two oak file cabinets occupied a corner next to a stacked bookcase with horizontal glass doors. A gun case held a collection of long guns on the opposite wall. Mounted next to it, in its own rack, was the lethal shape of a custom-made Winchester 1886 lever-action Sporting Rifle.

Ronnie made the introductions. During the formalities, Stark took his gauge of the wrangler's companions.

The pair were cut from the same sturdy cloth as Ronnie, although both had a few years on him. Stark typed them as small-time ranchers or stockmen, more at home working cattle or riding the range than spending time in the territorial capital confabbing with a high-priced troubleshooter. Like Ronnie, they wore their guns as if they were more tools than weapons.

Cass Bishop was broad as a bar ditch, but his brown, weathered face was amiable enough. Stu Hollingshed was taller and leaner, with the air of a man who has yet to be convinced.

Waving them to ladderback chairs in front of his

desk, Stark took his own oak swivel chair and rocked back in it as they got themselves seated.

"What can I do for you gentlemen?"

After a moment Bishop took up the role of spokesman, and he didn't bother beating around the bush. "You can shut down the varmint who's been hounding us near out of business."

"What business is that?"

"We're ranchers up in the Indian Lands, leasing pasture from the tribes," Bishop asserted. "None of us are real big time, but we get by. Me and Stu here raise some beef cattle. Ronnie runs some mustangs. And there's others like us, plenty of others. You might say we represent a good dozen ranchers. Leastways, that's how many are putting up the money to hire you."

"I don't work cheap."

"We know that."

"Fair enough. What seems to be the trouble?"

Stark was conscious of Hollingshed's skeptical gaze. Ronnie was sitting expectantly on the edge of his chair.

"Rustlers," Bishop said in answer to Stark's question. "They been hitting spreads our size mighty regular. They stay away from the bigger outfits like Andrew Blaine's. He's the one gave you a clean bill of health. And, of course, we heard how you wiped out Dirk Garland and his gang after Blaine sicced you on them."

"Rustling's nothing new in the Indian Lands," Stark commented. "Sort of goes with the territory. But you mentioned just one man."

Bishop nodded. ''That's right. If it was only small bands of rustlers hitting us, we could team up and likely run them to ground before they had time to haze our stock up to Liberal and Tyrone where they could sell them. But the way things stand, they don't have no need to drive them that far. Once they cross over into no-man's-land, this fellow we're after is ready to take the rustled stock off their hands for a song. When he accumulates a big enough herd, he runs it on north into Kansas and sells them at a fat profit. He handles altering any brands that need changing. Saves the rustlers themselves a heap of time and risk.''

''A cattle rustlers' broker,'' Stark mused. ''He must have a crew working for him.''

Bishop grunted affirmation. ''A sizable one, nigh onto twenty men, we reckon, most of them gun slicks and hardcases. There's no short supply of them in those parts. They're ramrodded by a shootist name of Tallant.''

Stark's eyebrows lifted. ''Sedge Tallant?''

''That'd be him. They stay holed up in a sort of stockade like a cavalry fort not far from a sorry sinkhole known as Sod Town where they go to carouse. Since the whole operation is in no-man's-land, there ain't a lawman anywhere can lay a finger on them. And they're too many for us to handle ourselves.''

Bishop's assessment of no-man's-land was on the money, Stark reflected. Disowned by both Texas and Kansas when they'd become states, the strip listed officially as the Unassigned Lands had ended up in a jurisdictional void, outside the authority of any official law enforcement agency. It was known as a haven for the godless breed.

"The hombre behind this scheme sounds like quite an operator," Stark surmised aloud. "Who is he?"

"A local businessman and restaurant owner right here in Guthrie," Bishop offered promptly. "Randall Burke."

"Well, now," Stark drawled. "You don't say."

"You know him?" Bishop guessed shrewdly.

"We've met," Stark allowed. The notion of Randall Burke running a rustling operation was an easy one to accept. The mental image of Burke whisking Prudence away to the dance floor prodded him like Mexican spurs. "You might say he tried to rustle something from me."

"Then you'll help us?"

"Yeah," Stark said. "I'll put his Indian Lands outfit out of business."

Ronnie slapped his thigh. "Yessir, I knew you were the man for the job after I seen you lay into those plug-uglies of Burke's last night!"

"Those were Burke's men?" Stark asked sharply.

"Yep. They followed me from the Golden Apple. I'd gone over there on my own to do a little snooping before we got together with you. Burke got suspicious and sent those yahoos after me."

Stark chewed it over. If Burke was alerted that there might be a move against him, it wouldn't make the job of rousting him any easier.

"Say you do stamp out his operation in no-man's-land," Hollingshed said by way of entering the conversation, leaning forward as he spoke, "what's to stop him from starting all over again up there? What can you do about that?'' His tone was truculent.

''He's not breaking any laws here,'' Stark pointed out.

''What's that got to do with it?'' Hollingshed demanded. ''You hire your gun out to the highest bidder, don't you?''

''Not when it puts me crossways with the law,'' Stark told him flatly. ''You boys need to remember a few things. I'm not a paid killer or a hired thug. I won't knowingly take a job that puts me afoul of the law, and there are some jobs I won't take regardless of whether or not they're legal.''

Hollingshed settled back in his chair with an air of bitter satisfaction. ''Ain't much need for hiring you then, as far as I can see.''

''That's up to you.'' Privately Stark admitted to himself that the rancher had a point. Bust up Burke's rustling ring in the Unassigned Lands, and, more than likely, he'd just start all over again and have it up and running before too much time was past.

''Stu, we beat this to death before we ever came to Guthrie.'' Bishop spoke up with an edge of anger. ''You don't want in, that's your right. But the rest of us are committed to hiring Mr. Stark. Way I look at it, we don't have a powerful lot in the way of choices.''

''Durn right!'' Ronnie added enthusiastically.

Hollingshed scowled at the other two men. He avoided looking at Stark. ''Okay,'' he said grudgingly. ''We'll give the Peacemaker his shot at it, for whatever good it will do us in the long run!''

Chapter Three

"Randall Burke?" U.S. Marshal Evett Nix echoed musingly. "Nope, I don't have anything on him. Word is, he cut a pretty wide swath with a six-gun down in Texas under a different name, but nothing's ever been pinned on him."

Nix turned away from his office window in the Herriott Building. He'd been standing there gazing out at the mix of traffic in the intersection of Division and Harrison Streets. Beneath his handlebar mustache his mouth was drawn in a shrewd line. "Why ask? Are you on to something?"

In his tailored suit, the head lawman for Oklahoma Territory looked to be more of a businessman than a marshal. And, in truth, it was his administrative skills that had earned him the appointment to the U.S. Marshal's office. But he'd rapidly gained the respect of the seasoned crew of veteran peace officers he'd recruited to ride under his authority.

Stark considered how to answer his question. He'd known it was coming, and he'd been giving it some thought since earlier that morning when his new clients had departed his office. Now he hitched his shoulders in a casual shrug. "Heard he's into some kind of cattle rustling setup in the Unassigned Lands."

"Even if it's true, there wouldn't be anything I could do about it. More's the pity. It's about time the government gave somebody jurisdiction over that benighted strip." Nix's tone sharpened. "You planning to go after him?"

"Not around here."

Nix regarded him steadily for a handful of seconds. "I'll hold you to that, Jim. You and I both know that you sometimes walk a trail right on the edge of the law. I've cut you a lot of slack, and even steered some business your way now and again because, most generally, the results you get benefit law and order. But I won't tolerate you going over that edge here in Guthrie, particularly when your target is a man who hasn't broken any laws in the territory. You read me?"

"Why, Evett, you know I'm a law-abiding man," Stark said easily. But despite his bantering tone, he didn't doubt a word that Nix said. If he locked horns with Burke on this turf, he'd be going up against the law as well.

"On the other hand," Nix relented a bit, "if you should come across something I need to know, then I'll expect you to bring it to me."

"You'll get chapter and verse," Stark assured him.

"Fair enough." Nix allowed himself a tight grin. "Good hunting."

They were parting on easy enough terms, Stark mused, but he'd have to step careful while he was under Nix's jurisdiction. For a moment he found himself wondering what Prudence would say if she knew of the job he'd taken on. He shrugged such musings aside.

Disgruntled, for reasons he didn't bother to ponder, he went in search of the handful of reliable contacts he had in certain odd corners and byways of Guthrie.

He didn't uncover anything worth keeping. ''Burke runs a clean operation,'' a saternine gambler known only as Ace confided to him. ''No rigged tables, no crooked dealing. It's enough to break a cardsharp's heart.''

That evening, Stark drifted into the Golden Apple's gambling hall through the street door. The night's crowd was already gathering. The murmur of voices and the clatter of roulette wheels rose through the muffling haze of tobacco smoke. Stark installed himself at the polished mahogany bar and ordered a beer. He sipped it once, then simply held the mug in his left hand. Only a fool dulled his senses and reflexes with alcohol.

He surveyed the room. Burke had a fancy layout, he acknowledged grudgingly. The furnishings were top-notch. An ornate pressed tin ceiling was overhead. Most of the customers were upper class, and even the bar girls, at first glance, looked to be ladies. Wheels of fortune and slot machines lined the walls. Stark noted setups for hazard, craps, keno, chuck-a-luck, and three-card monte. A half-dozen high-stakes poker games were in progress.

Where had Burke gotten the *dinero* to open this kind of establishment? Stark questioned. From his rustling crew in no-man's-land? It didn't seem likely. What else was the man involved in?

A little wire seemed to grow taut across his shoulders as he saw Burke's arrogant figure, ghosted by the silent Chin, wending through the ranks of customers toward him. Stark set the beer aside, hooked his right thumb in his gun belt just above the holstered Peacemaker, and watched them come. He was sure neither of the pair had missed the significance of his movement.

"Welcome back, Stark." Burke bared his teeth in a hard grin that was part challenge and part curiosity. "What brings you here a second night in a row?"

"Just out having a good time," Stark answered without inflection.

Burke snorted. "Not with Miss McKay, I see." He appraised Stark, then went on, "Looking for some company maybe? There are a few unattached women here tonight."

"Not interested." Stark read the disappointment in Burke's shifty eyes. The man was trying to read him and wasn't having any luck in deciphering what he saw.

"Care to try your luck then?" Burke gestured back at the gaming tables. "Always plenty of money to be won here."

"Or lost," Stark commented dryly. "Sorry, I'm not much of a betting man."

Burke's nostrils flared. "Maybe not on games of chance," he said with sudden shrewdness. "But how about betting on your own skills against those of another fighting man?"

Stark felt a predatory tingle dance down his spine. "Meaning you?"

Burke's grin was that of a man who has snared his

prey. "Not tonight." He tossed his head toward his silent bodyguard. "Chin here is who I had in mind."

"I'm listening."

"Well, I hear you can do some pretty fancy fighting tricks with your feet."

"Nothing special," Stark demurred.

"Chin learned something like your brand of fighting over in his native land. He was a bodyguard for the Emperor of China until he killed another bodyguard in a duel and had to flee the country. Killed him with his bare hands. He ended up in New York. I picked him up in Chinatown when I was back East arranging the finances for this place. No boasting, he can throw a punch or sling a throwing ax faster than a man can pull a gun. I've seen him do it."

Stark had tangled with the hatchetmen of the Chinese tongs when he'd worked for the Pinkertons. Deadly killers all, whether armed with the twin throwing axes they favored, or just their naked hands. He wasn't surprised that Chin was trained in the same killing arts. He had a hunch, though, that Chin would put to shame any of the paid assassins of the New York tongs.

"What've you got in mind?" he prodded Burke along.

"A little demonstration." Burke's voice was tight with eagerness. "Your skills against Chin's. I'll wager he's got moves you can't match with all your fancy foot fighting."

"Wager how much?" Stark drawled.

"Let's make it interesting. Five twenty-dollar gold pieces." Burke produced the coins as if by sleight of hand. With an air of challenge he laid them one by one on the bar.

Deliberately Stark produced five coins of his own and set them in a neat stack beside Burke's wager. Burke smiled as if he'd already won them, and wheeled toward the crowded room.

"Ladies and Gentlemen," he said, raising his voice to command attention above the clamor. Heads turned and the clatter subsided. "We have an exhibition arranged here, an exhibition and a wager. A contest of skills between two top-notch fighting men. Perhaps some of you would like to venture some money yourselves."

Burke was working the crowd like a professional showman, Stark mused.

"Two-to-one on the Peacemaker!" a man's voice called.

In moments Burke had his barkeeps booking the bets from the noisy crowd as he extolled the skills of his bodyguard over those of the "renowned Oklahoma troubleshooter."

Stark dismissed the hubbub from his mind. For the first time he turned his full attention on his opponent. Chin likewise appeared oblivious to the furor centering around the pair of them. He was watching Stark with an air of almost idle repose, his lean body loose and slack beneath his cheap oversize suit.

His thin lips moved, and Stark barely caught the soft-spoken words. "You are warrior."

Stark hitched his shoulders. "I guess we'll see."

Chin shook his head, and Stark wasn't sure what to make of that response. He wondered how the odds were running. Hopefully his backers wouldn't be disappointed in his performance.

Burke had cleared an area from in front of the bar. A half-circle of expectant faces hemmed Chin and Stark into their makeshift stage. Burke, playing the moment, paced deliberately to the bar and picked up one of the gold coins he'd placed there. He turned his head toward his servant.

Chin stepped farther into the open area. Stark eyed him closely, noting the lazy tension beginning to coil in his movements. With no further signal Burke flipped the coin toward him. Chin plucked it deftly out of the air with a flicker of his hand.

For a moment Chin stood motionless, arms at his sides. His shoulders lifted as he inhaled. Has face bore no more expression than the mahogany bar. Then his head turned in a peculiar little cocking movement, and he snapped the gold coin spinning up and away from him. As it fell, his entire form whirled into a high, twirling leap. In midair, as his body came around, one leg snapped out like a whip.

Stark had only a fraction of a heartbeat to realize what was coming, but even his trained eye couldn't quite see that lashing foot intercept the falling coin. There was a gleaming flash of motion, then a small solid sound of impact at the far end of the large room. Chin came out of the leaping kick in a crouching stance, one arm arced overhead, the other outthrust before him.

"By Godfrey, it's stuck in the wall!" a man's hoarse voice cried.

Stark squinted. Sure enough, the gold coin, pro-

Clifford Blair

pelled by the power of Chin's kick, was half embedded in the soft plaster of the wall. An amazed murmur ran through the crowd, and there was a shifting toward the spot as the spectators sought confirmation with their own eyes. Gracefully Chin uncoiled from his stance.

It was a carny trick, a sideshow stunt, but it proved Burke hadn't been boasting about his servant's skills.

"Don't touch that coin!" Burke shouted as a drummer reached for it. The fellow jerked his hand back.

Gradually the attention of the crowd returned to Stark. Burke's teeth were bared in triumph. Past his burly shoulder, Stark could see Chin. The Chinaman's face was impassive, but his eyes were flat and hard in challenge.

"Well, Mr. Stark?" Burke demanded. "Take your turn if you care to."

Stark gave a thoughtful shake of his head. "Your man's mighty good," he admitted laconically. "Appears as how I'm purely outclassed." As he spoke he took two sauntering steps toward a fine wooden poker table. "Yessir," he added, "outclassed."

With the final word he swung one stiffened leg up and brought the heel of his boot smashing down full into the center of the table, his breath bursting from him in a bark of effort. The solid two-inch boards splintered like shoddy shingles under the blunt end of an ax, and the table buckled into a pile of kindling.

Stark wheeled smoothly away. Burke was gaping. Chin had recoiled slightly, as if about to draw back into his fighting stance once again.

"This ought to cover the damages." Stark thumbed another gold piece from his pocket. "Here."

He gave it a gentle toss, then stepped swiftly forward as it fell. His knee lifted and his foot hinged out to catch the tumbling coin and send it shooting upward. It rang off the pressed tin ceiling like the ricochet of a bullet, and every head in the room ducked except Stark's.

"Next time I'll make the rules," Stark promised, and strode past Burke and out the door.

His nerves were stretched taut as guitar strings, and his hand ached for the butt of his Colt, but he kept going without casting a look back.

A block from the Golden Apple he sidestepped swiftly into the darkened mouth of an alley, made two more turns, then halted in the shadows, waiting. Minutes went by. He heard the sound of men's voices, but they passed. Hurdy-gurdy music drifted toward him.

He let himself relax a little. If Stace and his pards, or some other hirelings of Burke, had followed him from the Golden Apple, then he'd lost them. If Chin had been on his tail, it might've been a different matter. He recalled the flashing speed and devastating power of the Chinese killer, and felt tautness creep back into his muscles.

He was still wary as he made his way to his hotel. Only when he was safely in his suite of rooms did he feel comfortable in undoing his gun belt. By habit he kept the little .38 close at hand.

He'd learned a bit about his enemy, he reflected. But by way of trade-off, he might've alerted Burke to his interest in his affairs. On the whole he wasn't sure he was happy with the outcome. Like his contest with Chin, he might've made a bad bet.

He shrugged such concerns aside. Not much point in fretting about it now. Resolutely he set about cleaning his guns before he hit the hay. He wanted a good night's sleep.

Tomorrow he'd head for no-man's-land.

Chapter Four

Stark rode into Sod Town with misgivings gnawing at his gut. He was armed for bear, with six-gun and bowie knife sheathed at his waist, and the .38 hideout gun snugly in place. Both the Winchester ten-gauge lever-action shotgun he favored, and the 50-110 Express Sporting Rifle he'd recently acquired, rode in scabbards on his saddle.

But though he was ready for trouble, he wasn't looking for it. Not yet, at any rate.

He'd made the trip to no-man's-land by rail and horseback. For the past two days he'd been riding through the rugged plains country in a realm where lawlessness was the rule, and few were the men who could be trusted.

Sod Town, where Burke's hardcases were said to carouse, was just the kind of low-life community you'd expect the Unassigned Lands to spawn, he mused grimly as he sat his big sorrel stallion and surveyed the place with a sour eye. The notorious Chitwood gang had run their horse thieving operation out of here until they'd been lynched.

The town might've grown up raggedly from the prairie itself. There wasn't a permanent building in it. Every structure was built out of blocks of sod that had

33

been hewn out of the hard earth to form crude, make-shift bricks. Even in place in the walls some of the blocks still had buffalo grass growing out of them, like patches of fur on the mangy hide of a dog. Given time, the relentless wind and seasonal torrential rains would dissolve the the place back into the dirt from which it had come.

Trash and debris littered the rutted tracks that served as streets. Among the motley collection of structures Stark could pick out a store, a blacksmith shop, a café, and a couple of saloons. It was these last two that caught his interest. Hipshot horses with battered hulls on their backs were tied in front of both establishments.

He gigged the sorrel forward. A ragged group of boys, varying in age from youngsters to teenagers, emerged from a shack as he drew near. A handful of them carried books or tablets. The older ones wore holstered pistols as if they were no strangers to their use. They studied Stark warily as he came abreast. A haggard man with a gaunt face and a book in his hand stood framed for a moment in the doorway of the shack. It was afternoon, and school was just letting out, Stark realized. Killers started out young here. He kept a wary eye of his own on the youths after he'd passed them by.

His misgivings grew. He'd planned on drifting in here to test the breeze before he actually set out to stalk his prey. But some of the sorrier denizens of Sod Town might well recognize his face. Word that the Peacemaker was hereabouts could spread fast, and it might get Sedge Tallant, Burke's gun boss, wondering what brought him here.

Irritably Stark tamped his concerns down. Odds were no one would know him from any other gun slick riding through. And odds were he wouldn't be running into Tallant himself. If he did, it was bad news, because Tallant was sure to recognize him. They knew each other from a ways back. . . .

But the risk was worth it, he calculated. The more he could learn about Burke's setup before he tied into it, the better his chances would be.

He stepped down from the sorrel in front of the nearest saloon. He had an odd moment when he wondered what Prudence McKay would think if she saw him at that moment. He'd left Guthrie without seeing her again, and he figured he'd be back in plenty of time to play expert witness for her. So why in tarnation did he feel like he'd committed some trespass in not informing her of his plans? His comings and goings were no concern of hers.

The saloon wasn't inviting. Heavy stones atop the board roof held it in place against the rangeland winds. The sagging door stood open, revealing only a black maw. Stark's nostrils twisted involuntarily at the heavy odor of waste and despair wafting out of its squalid depths.

He brushed the butt of his .45 with trailing fingers, then set his shoulders and swung through the door, sidestepping almost immediately so he wouldn't be framed against the daylight.

The interior of the dive wasn't much more than a dirt cave. Lanterns, their chimneys begrimed by smoke, provided a dim illumination. Chinks in the roof and the sod walls let in a little more light. A bar, made up of planks nailed to barrels, took up one side of the room. A mismatched collection of tables cluttered most of the rest of the space. Scattered among the tables were a dozen or so men.

There was a general turning of heads and shifting of positions at Stark's entry. He felt them trying to appraise him; they were of the breed that looked on every stranger as a likely enemy.

Stark crossed to the bar. He moved like one of them, and he sensed a subtle lessening of the tension. The barkeep had a six-gun stuck in the apron that encircled his bulging gut. He looked as mean as his patrons.

''Beer,'' Stark said.

The barkeep waited until he put a coin on the rough-hewn plank before he complied. The coin disappeared in a scarred fist.

Stark took only a sip of the tepid brew. That was all. He sure didn't want to dull his senses or reflexes in this den of thieves. Mug in hand, he drifted to an unoccupied table in the gloom of a corner and planted himself in a rickety chair. He felt the head of a nail dig into him, and hitched his leg into a different position.

The slight commotion caused by his arrival was fading. Apparently no one had recognized him, or if anyone had, they were keeping it to themselves for reasons of their own. Peering out from under the brim of his Stetson, Stark made his own appraisal of the room's occupants.

The faces of a few of them he knew from the file

of Wanted circulars he kept back at his office in Guthrie. Here were bounties on the hoof if he'd been out to collect them. Silently he pondered how many of this bunch rode for Burke.

The mutter of voices grew more relaxed. A couple of sluggish poker games were going on. A used-up bar girl was joshing a cowpoke at one of the tables. Not even the poor light or the hazy atmosphere could make her pretty again. The cowpoke didn't seem to mind.

Stark toyed with the mug and let the murmured words and hushed tones of the other patrons drift to him. He was pretty much ignored. They'd accepted him as one of their own. He wondered what it said about him that he could fit in so easily with ruthless, violent men.

After a spell he stretched his legs out and let his chin sag to his chest like a hunted man relaxing for the first time in days. But his eyes and ears remained alert.

Most of this pack were drifters, saddle tramps, and two-bit outlaws. They weren't the caliber of hands a top gun boss like Sedge Tallant would want riding for him. The exception was a hard-bitten trio sharing a bottle of whiskey at a table across the room. They were cut from a tougher cloth than the rest.

Stark couldn't overhear much of what was said, but he caught a muttered reference to ". . . the boys riding for the big outfit" from a closer table. The remark seemed to refer to the three hardcases.

The afternoon squirmed past like a lazy sidewinder. Daylight from the open doorway crept farther into the dark interior of the saloon. A few of the saddle tramps drifted out. Stark heard the clatter of departing hooves. He turned down an affable offer to join one of the poker games, not wanting to risk recognition by closer contact with any of the players. After that he was left alone.

Another floozy appeared from somewhere and joined the three gunmen and the whiskey. They ordered a fresh bottle, and things got a little livelier at their table. Stark pricked up his ears, but caught nothing of interest.

He was giving serious contemplation to moseying over to the other saloon when the pound of hooves on the rutted street brought his head up a bit. In a moment he heard the sound of men's voices and glimpsed motion through the entryway. Casually he hooked his thumb in his gun belt and watched the door with hooded eyes.

A handful of men jostled their way into the saloon, calling out rowdy greetings to the three hardcases sharing the bottle with the bar girl. The newcomers all had the same lawless stamp to them.

One of them in particular stepped clear of the door and took his time surveying the room, just as Stark himself had done. Stark felt his hackles bristle.

The newcomer was a big horse-faced man with the awkward, gangly build of a newborn colt. But there was nothing gangly or awkward about the catlike way he moved, or the speed with which, Stark knew, he could handle the revolver strapped low on his hip. Silently Stark berated himself for not having ridden out sooner, or better yet, having been fool enough to stop here in the first place.

The rawboned man spotted Stark as a stranger within a dozen seconds of entering the dirt room. For a moment his big shape was very still. It was too dim for quick recognition. He took a couple of deliberate paces nearer, squinting through the haze.

"Hold it, boys." He cut off his companions' palaver without taking his eyes from Stark's half-reclining form. "I'll be hanged if we don't have the Peacemaker himself gracing us with his company."

That got their attention, and that of everybody else in the place. There was a price for notoriety, Stark thought darkly, and it looked like he was about to have to pay it.

"Howdy, Sedge," he drawled.

Sedge Tallant moved closer. He was careful to keep out of range of Stark's booted feet. His silhouette blotted out the light from the doorway. Stark stayed where he was. Drawing from his position might slow him a little bit, but the table and chairs gave him some shelter that he wouldn't have if he was standing on his feet.

"What brings you to this neck of the woods, Stark?" Tallant growled.

"Sedge, you know it ain't polite to ask a man that in these parts," Stark chided gently, then let his tone harden. "Besides, my business is none of your concern."

Tallant wasn't committed to action just yet, but he looked ready for it. The big knuckles of his hand dangled even with his Colt. Stark's own six-shooter rode higher on his hip, but he knew the gun boss was plenty fast even with a holster that was worn too low. Maybe faster than the Peacemaker himself.

"Could be you and me got unfinished business," Tallant stated carefully. "Last time we crossed paths up in Meridian, you took one of my boys in to be hung before I ever knew you hit town. I didn't cotton to that then, and I don't cotton to you being here now."

Tallant's men had shifted so that pretty near all of them would have a clear field of fire at Stark if it came to gunplay. Stark counted eight of them, including the trio at the table and Tallant himself. It was going to take the grace of God for him to walk out of here alive.

"Your boy needed hanging to straighten him out," Stark said with heavy irony. "You know that. He was loco—killed a settler and his whole family just so he could steal their only horse. I did you a favor taking him off your hands."

Tallant gave a horse's snort. "Don't reckon I need your favors, Stark. If a man in my outfit has to be brought to rein, I'll do it."

Stark hitched his shoulders a fraction. "Nothing personal." His back was starting to ache from the tension gripping the muscles at the base of his spine.

"I'm still wondering what brings you up this way," Tallant prodded.

"Just passing through." Stark relented enough to give him an answer. He used his chin to indicate the gunsels backing Tallant. "Looks like you're sitting pretty; all these fine, upstanding gentlemen riding under you."

Another nasal snort. ''Pretty enough to where I don't want you hereabouts. I got bigger irons in the fire than worrying about settling our differences. Killing you might stir up all sorts of ruckus.''

''Just getting it done in the first place might too,'' Stark commented coolly. He was standing his ground now. His hard-earned reputation demanded it. He couldn't afford to back down completely, not even against odds like these. Not even if it meant his death.

''Oh, we'd get the job done, right enough.'' Tallant wasn't the sort to crawfish either. ''But if you're only riding through, then we won't hold you up none. Anyways, what's between you and me is best settled one on one.''

''Maybe another day,'' Stark agreed.

Gingerly he drew his legs back and rose slowly to his feet, keeping his hand near his holster. When he stood erect, the butt of his Colt was even with his forearm. There was additional shifting among Tallant's crew, but no sudden movements.

Stark ran a practiced eye over them. More bounties on the hoof. If this was a fair sample of the men Tallant had under his brand, then Randall Burke was paying top-gun wages. Putting this pack out of business wouldn't be easy.

Tallant eased from his path as Stark edged sideward toward the door, trying to keep the gun boss and all his men within range of his vision. It couldn't be done. He didn't like the feeling. He didn't like a lot about this setup.

''Hey, Stark.'' Tallant's voice stopped him in the doorway. ''You still packing that repeating shotgun?''

"Yep," Stark confirmed. "Don't send anybody after me, or they'll get a taste of it."

"Like you said, maybe another day. Right now, we're not getting paid to fight you."

Not yet, Stark added silently, and walked out of the saloon into the fading daylight. *Grace of God,* he thought fervently.

Chapter Five

Despite his warning, somebody was following him, Stark realized as he put Sod Town behind him in the lengthening afternoon. It was something he sensed more than saw. But once, casting a quick glance back, he caught a glimpse of what might've been a mounted figure disappearing behind one of the grassy hillocks of this rolling prairie country.

Whoever it was had a certain skill, he acknowledged. The mysterious rider was staying to the low ground, circling bluffs instead of cresting them. But it was puzzling that Tallant had sent only one man.

Well, he'd given them fair warning, Stark reflected ruefully. It looked like hostilities might have to commence a little sooner than he'd planned.

When chance offered, he turned the sorrel swiftly into the mouth of a shadowed draw. "Easy, Red," he murmured, and the big stallion stood rigid under him.

Tallant had asked him about his shotgun. He unshipped it now. He'd gained a healthy appreciation for the 1887 ten-gauge, lever-action repeating shotgun with its four-shell capacity and thirty-two-inch barrel. Its stopping power, even at a respectable range, made it preferable, in Stark's mind, to the more common repeating rifles with their greater magazine capacity.

He alternated solid lead slugs with .00 buckshot in his loads, and he carried extra shells in the bandolier he'd slipped on after leaving the saloon.

For really long-range work he had the big Sporting Rifle, but this current confrontation didn't promise to be long range. . . .

Shotgun cradled in his arms, the barrel leveled casually at the mouth of the draw, he waited.

After a handful of minutes he heard the rustle of hooves in the buffalo grass. The fingers of his right hand curled into the lever action. His left tightened on the barrel. A rider hove into view before him.

Stark's teeth ground together at sight of the familiar wiry figure. ''What the blazes are you doing here?'' he gritted.

Ronnie Hall reined up sharply and swiveled about in his saddle. His boyish face went wide with shock. ''Mr. Stark!'' he stammered.

Stark worked the shotgun's lever with an angry snap of his wrist. ''Speak up!''

''I . . . I was following you. Thought I might give you a hand.''

''You're lucky you didn't get your fool head blown off!''

Ronnie stilled his mount expertly. It figured to be one of his string—a steel gray mustang as rangy and tough as its rider. ''I didn't mean no harm. Like I said, I reckoned I might be able to help.''

''You figured wrong. I work alone.'' Stark's tone was flat.

Ronnie nodded somberly. He looked so dispirited that Stark eased up, tilting the barrel of the shotgun skyward. Warily he glanced about to be sure his preoccupation with the young bronc buster hadn't left him vulnerable to some other foe. Satisfied, he turned his attention back to Ronnie.

''Where'd you pick me up?'' he queried in an easier tone. Some relief showed on Ronnie's face. He jerked his head over his shoulder. ''Back yonder at Sod Town. You told us in Guthrie this would likely be your first stop, so I figured I'd just be waiting for you. Turns out, you beat me there, but I was up in the hills waiting when I saw you come out of the saloon.''

''Why hang on my backtrail? Why not sing out first?''

Ronnie hung his head sheepishly. ''Wasn't sure you'd want me along.''

Stark scowled as he cleared the chamber and thumbed the shell back into the magazine. He returned the shotgun to its scabbard. ''You got that right,'' he said bluntly. ''I play a lone hand. You'd just get in my way.''

Ronnie's jaw jutted stubbornly. ''I can lead you right to Burke's compound,'' he asserted. ''I've scouted the whole area since this started, and they've never laid eyes on me to suspect I was anything but a stray cowpoke.''

Stark regarded him thoughtfully. ''You did do a right fair job of trailing me,'' he admitted grudgingly.

''I've hunted wild mustangs in these hills and elsewhere since I was knee-high to an antelope. A man who can sneak up on a herd of horses, pick the one he wants, and drop a loop on it, can sure ride rings around most hombres without them ever knowing it.''

A look of chagrin crossed Ronnie's face. "I'm kind of surprised you spotted me."

Stark shrugged. "You hunt horses. I hunt men." He nodded at the pistol worn too far back on Ronnie's hip. "You any good with that six-shooter or that long gun you're packing?"

"I can fight," Ronnie said.

"Didn't ask that. Have you ever used either of those irons against another man?"

"Traded shots with a couple of yahoos looking to cut some of the best stock out of my herd. They high-tailed it."

That was something in the kid's favor anyway. Stark continued to regard him skeptically.

"I wouldn't get in your way, Mr. Stark."

"The name's Jim," Stark supplied absently. He chewed it over. There was no reason not to believe the young man. A scheme like this seemed right in line with his reading of Ronnie's character. The mustanger could ride, and he knew this region, and he wasn't looking for bloodshed. Now that Tallant was alerted of the Peacemaker's presence in the area, it might not hurt to have another set of eyes and ears, and an extra gun.

"You do what I tell you," he ordered. "If I can use you, I will. If you're in the way, then I send you packing. If I can't put you to use then you just keep quiet. Savvy?"

Ronnie grinned eagerly. "You're calling the shots."

Stark held his gaze a moment longer. Ronnie didn't flinch.

''Let's drift,'' Stark said. ''We been camped out here long enough.''

With dusk, Stark mounted a ridge and lay flat on his belly, using his fine German field glasses to search their backtrail methodically. He spotted a couple of distant horsemen, but they seemed intent on business of their own, and he dismissed them.

Sod Town was some miles behind them, and he'd deliberately swung wide of the direct route to Burke's compound. Ronnie had seemed as good as his word. He'd said little and followed Stark's lead unswervingly. Stark began to feel a little better about having him along.

They made camp in the shelter of a high bluff. Stark built a smokeless fire long enough to fix beans and bacon and coffee. Then he smothered the flames. Ronnie didn't protest, he noted with approval. The night would be cool, but the fewer signs they made of their presence the safer they were. A campfire flame could be seen for a goodly distance at night. Here every man's hand must be counted against them.

''What about standing guard?'' the wrangler asked as Stark freed his bedroll.

''Red'll take care of it.'' Stark gave a nod in the direction of the sorrel he'd hobbled nearby.

''Good piece of horseflesh,'' Ronnie commented.

They talked horses for a spell. Ronnie knew his trade, right enough, Stark concluded. He was no stranger to horses himself.

Coyotes began to yip and howl at the stars and at one another. From farther off, the deeper, mournful wail of a wolf silenced the coyotes for a time. Another lobo answered the first. The wolves were gathering. Four-legged predators, as well as two-legged ones, prowled these grasslands.

"How'd you and Bishop and Hollingshed learn about Burke's setup?" Stark queried.

"There'd been rumors about it, and then one day we caught a pair of wide-loopers red-handed," Ronnie recounted. "They talked plenty; told us all about how Burke worked things; where his headquarters is; and how much a head he paid for stock. They even knew the name of his restaurant in Guthrie." The mustanger's voice hardened as he spoke.

Stark didn't ask what had become of the hapless rustlers. He knew what fate awaited them at the hands of the ranchers whose stock they'd been plundering. Courtrooms and lawyers were a long way away out here. So were jails. A quick noose would've been their sentence.

"You've seen the compound?" he probed further.

"Yep," Ronnie announced proudly. "I rode up to take a gander at it. Pretended to be a saddle tramp who just happened onto it. I got a look, sure enough, but a couple of outriders threw down on me almost as soon as I did." Ronnie gave a slow shake of his head. Stark couldn't see his face in the darkness. "I did some wondering if they were going to let me ride away from there alive."

So the rustling headquarters was well guarded. Stark wasn't surprised. Whether on Burke's orders, or acting on his own, Sedge Tallant would've taken that precaution. Stark said as much aloud.

"Just who is this Tallant hombre?" Ronnie wanted to know.

"A top gun boss," Stark answered shortly. "He specializes in organizing or ramrodding packs of gun slicks working for gun wages. Takes a special talent to hold men like that together for very long. And Tallant's no slouch when it comes to handling a shooting iron himself."

"Faster than you?" Ronnie blurted, then looked sorry he'd asked.

"Good question," Stark said soberly, then changed the subject. "I want us within a couple of miles of that compound before daylight," he advised. "I plan on having a look-see at it myself."

"I can get us right in close before the sun's up," Ronnie boasted.

"Just get me within a couple of miles. Then I'll be going in on foot." Stark sensed Ronnie's shock. For most horsemen the idea of hiking someplace when a horse could do the traveling for you was a purely foreign notion.

But Ronnie offered no objection when Stark rousted him out of his bedroll while there was still plenty of night to spare. For breakfast they gnawed on jerky as Ronnie led the way cautiously across the plains. At length he reined up.

"I calculate the compound to be about two miles west of here," he advised softly. "You'll have the sun at your back like you wanted.

Stark nodded approval. A man looking into the rising sun was a lot less likely to spot an intruder on his range.

In the shelter of a deep arroyo they dismounted. "Stay put here if you can until after dark tonight," Stark instructed. "If I'm not back by then, you're on your own. Leave my horse and go back to our camp. Give me another day, then go home. Whatever happens, don't come in there after me. If I run into trouble, I'll make it out as best I can. If you're not here when I get back, I'll find you if I need to. *Comprende?*"

The mustanger nodded.

Stark stepped out of the saddle. Methodically he shucked his boots and donned his high Apache moccasins. They made traveling afoot quieter and a mite easier than hobbling around in horseman's footgear. With the shotgun slung over his shoulder, he took a last appraising glance at the younger man.

"Be seeing you," he said.

Ronnie cleared his throat. "Keep an eye peeled for them outriders. I reckon they make their rounds at night too."

Stark didn't answer. He disappeared into the darkness. Behind him he thought he heard Ronnie gasp at the swiftness of his going.

The terrain in no-man's-land alternated between flat prairie, gentle, rolling hills, and the kind of rugged up-and-down country in which he now prowled. Except along the banks of creeks, or in riverbeds, trees were few and far between. For cover, he was forced to rely on the narrow draws, deep defiles, and grassy arroyos that snaked through the leg-straining hillocks. The thick buffalo grass made walking a chore, but the clumps gave him purchase and handholds in climbing some of the steeper slopes.

At night it was less risky to skyline himself, but he still took few chances. He kept his ears and nostrils open. Sound or smell were likely to alert him before his eyes could discern much in the gloom.

The sky overhead was clear. The stars were sharp gleaming shards of crystal. Occasionally he heard the whisper of wings as some night bird swooped low. Once, a coyote set to yipping from so close atop a ridge that it startled him. A slight breeze brushed past him.

Eventually that breeze carried the crackle of men's voices to him, as well as the sweat scent of horseflesh. Like a revenant returning to the grave, Stark sank down into the thick grass, shrugging his shotgun into his hand as he did so. He pressed himself flat and waited.

The pair of outriders went by some ten yards in front of him. Their disgruntled tones reached him clearly.

"Durn fool business riding guard this far out in the dead of night. Who does Tallant think is going to be sneaking up on us out here? Ain't been any hostile Indians in these parts for years."

"He's a careful man." The first speaker's pard wasn't as eager to disparage their boss. "Besides, this beats pushing cattle north to Kansas. And you heard Tallant say they ran into the Peacemaker over to Sod Town."

"The Peacemaker! Haw! He's just another hombre

packing a rep that's bigger than his gun. What could one man do to this outfit anyway?''

His companion kept his own counsel.

Stark grinned coldly. He could've emptied the saddles of these two particular members of the outfit with a single load of buckshot, but now was too soon to start thinning their ranks. But come a day before too long, and he'd show this doubting Thomas just what the Peacemaker could do to his sorry outfit.

When the riders had faded away into the night, Stark ghosted forward. Dawn would be coming soon, and he wanted to have a secure vantage point before then. But he couldn't afford to trade caution for haste.

Twice more he evaded pairs of outriders. At least three sets of them were patrolling the night range. Likely there were others. Tallant was taking his job seriously. If his mounted guards had taken their tasks just as seriously, then Stark's work would've been a good deal harder. But these were hired guns, not military men. They were dangerous enough, but even a gun boss like Tallant couldn't whip too much discipline out of them.

At length, with dawn brightening the eastern skyline at his back, he heard the lowing of cattle and caught the mingled odors of a large encampment of men. He spotted a human figure standing sentry duty on a craggy overlook, but slipped by easy enough. Another chance to thin their ranks not taken, he thought ruefully. But if he had his way, Tallant and his minions wouldn't know he'd been here this time.

He took cover atop a steep-sided hogback, squirming into a thorny thicket that would conceal him from the casual eye and dissuade any searcher from probing too hard.

Gingerly, wincing at the occasional bite of a thorn, he unlimbered his field glasses and got his first good look at Burke's compound.

Chapter Six

Whoever had laid out the headquarters for Burke's rustling operation—Stark suspected it had been Burke himself—had done a professional job. The compound was little short of a defensive fortress, with an eight-foot palisade enclosing several acres of a wide, flat plain. There were a couple of bunkhouses and storage sheds, as well as a barn and a stable.

In the center of the compound, a twenty-foot watch-tower had been erected. It wasn't fancy, but a lookout stationed there would have a commanding view of the surrounding countryside. And even at this early hour of morning it was already manned, Stark noted.

Holding pens for the rustled beeves were outside the walls. The pens were currently full. If any more stolen stock was brought in, it would have to be held outside the pens where the buffalo grass would make good pasture. A windmill, blades turning lazily in the morning breeze, provided fresh well water. Stark shook his head in silent admiration.

Careful to keep his field glasses shielded, even though the rising sun was at his back, Stark continued his scrutiny. Several men were handling chores in a lackadaisical fashion. Others loafed about near what was undoubtedly a mess hall and cookshack, waiting for morning grub. Stark smelled the faint scents of coffee and bacon. His stomach growled at him.

Double gates were set on opposite sides of the fort. Both were open, but it wouldn't take long to get them secured. Once they were closed, the outlaws would have a defensible site that might cause even trained soldiers to balk at a frontal assault.

But Stark wasn't planning to tackle the place head-on.

He held his position as the sun rose higher. Eventually the heat found its way down into the thicket and seemed to become trapped there by the thorns. Sweat beaded on Stark's forehead and traced a path down into his eyebrows until he had to lower the binoculars and sleeve his eyes clear.

He couldn't get a satisfactory head count in the fortress. Tallant and the other hardcases who'd been with him in Sod Town had returned to the hideout at some point. Stark saw the gun boss issuing orders to a group of yahoos lounging about. None of them disputed his authority, and soon the chores were being handled with a little more alacrity.

Tallant himself mounted the watchtower and joined the lookout on the small roofed platform. Taking the man's field glasses, the gun boss spent a goodly amount of time scanning the countryside. Stark lowered his head and tried to sink down into the earth itself as the glasses passed slowly over his place of concealment. He fancied he could evade Tallant's experienced gaze probing the intervening tangle of branches. He drew a sigh of relief as Tallant swung the glasses on in his methodical circuit.

Was the gun boss just practicing ordinary caution? Or was he being extra wary since the Peacemaker was in the region?

At length Tallant returned the glasses to the lookout and clambered easily down from the tower. He disappeared into a small cabin, probably housing his living quarters.

A young blond woman in a homespun dress emerged from the cookshack to empty a pail of soapy water. Oddly, none of the nearby rowdies offered to bother her. She was the cook, Stark supposed. But somehow she seemed out of place.

When she went back into the mess hall Stark decided he had seen enough. The longer he remained here, the greater the chance of discovery. A true surveillance of the compound would take too long and involve too much risk. He'd make do with what information he'd already gleaned.

Carefully he wriggled free from the thicket and began his withdrawal from the vicinity. He'd deliberately worn trail clothes faded and weathered until they were nearly colorless. They blended well with the muted colors of the prairie. Daylight made it easier for him to be spotted, but it also made it easier for him to pick out a route that kept him out of sight except from some luckless guard who might stumble upon him.

None did. He stayed low, working his way around hills and buttes, never skylining himself, keeping to the draws and arroyos whenever he could. Once he jumped a big jackrabbit, later a coyote. Each time he waited to be sure the animal's flight hadn't drawn attention before he moved on.

Pronghorn antelope played and grazed on distant hillsides. A pair of hawks circled high overhead, watching for prey of their own. Long gone were the days of the buffalo which had once thrived in this land. Stark found himself questioning whether Ronnie had stayed put where he'd left him.

But the mustanger was awaiting him when he slipped into the draw. Ronnie started at Stark's appearance, although the younger man had clearly kept an eye out for trouble.

"You move like a consarned puma!" he complained.

"Reckon you do the same when you're hunting horses," Stark pointed out. Privately he was even more pleased with his companion's performance. Time would tell if Ronnie could hunt men as well as he hunted horses.

Stark deemed it safe to mount their horses when they pulled back farther from the outlaw base. At a distance they would be taken only as another pair of saddle tramps drifting through the grasslands.

As they rode, he described in some detail what he'd seen. "It's a good layout," he concluded. "Won't be easy to breach."

"I got a look at it once myself," Ronnie commented. "But I sure didn't see what you did. You noticed a heap of things I missed."

"I know what I'm looking for. I've been doing this sort of thing for a long time," Stark replied.

They rode on a little ways, then Ronnie cocked his head toward Stark. "Why do you do it?" he asked abruptly. "Make your living with a gun, I mean. You ain't like the killers Burke hires."

Stark ceased his relentless scanning of the countryside to cast an eye at the wrangler. "Why do you raise horses and work at catching and breaking mustangs?"

"I guess because I'm good at it, and I like to do it."

Stark nodded. "There you go."

"But I ain't running the risk of getting shot every time I take on a job," Ronnie protested.

"You're running the risk of getting stove up, or worse, by some loco bronc."

Ronnie chewed it over for a moment. "All right, I'll grant you that." His chin lifted with a trace of defiance. "But what I do doesn't involve killing people."

Stark looked over his shoulder at his backtrail. Nothing there that he could see. Ronnie's voice hadn't held accusation, only an honest effort to fathom the makeup of the man he rode with. The question he'd put was nothing new to Stark. He'd heard it before in one fashion or another, sometimes voiced with a lot more hostility. And he'd had this same conversation with a lot of folks. How could a God-fearing man make a living spilling the blood of other men? He wasn't sure he had an answer yet himself.

"I sidestep killing when I can," he said, not defensively, just stating a fact. "And, as best I can, I try to stay inside the law. But sometimes fighting is necessary; sometimes killing is too. And lots of times there are decent upright folk who need someone to do their fighting for them and see that justice gets done. You and the other ranchers who hired me are examples. I'm better at fighting and handling a gun than I am at anything else. Good or bad, that's how I'll leave my mark when I'm gone. I figure to leave that mark on the side of justice. And, as for getting paid for what I do, even the Good Book says a laborer is worthy of his hire.''

Ronnie let it ride. His young, weatherbeaten face was lined with thought. Stark looked behind them again. He recalled his doubts that he was going to be able to handle this job without bending or breaking his own rule of operating within the law.

He called a halt at a small creek bordered by sheltering cottonwoods. The horses drank thirstily. Stark eyed Ronnie curiously.

''You're wearing your gun belt different,'' he commented.

Ronnie shifted his feet uncomfortably. ''Yeah, a little bit.''

At some point the wrangler had shifted his holster so that, like Stark's, it rode level with the middle of his forearm when his arm hung free.

''You tried pulling it from there?'' Stark inquired mildly.

''Some, while I was waiting for you this morning.''

''Let's see how you do. Don't try for speed. Just show me how you draw. Don't fire.''

Ronnie licked his lips, then hunched into an awkward crouch, arm crooked at his side. Despite Stark's injunction, he tried for speed, gripping the pistol with a clawed hand and yanking the weapon free. The barrel wobbled all over the compass before he got it leveled.

Self-consciously Ronnie holstered the pistol and looked apprehensively at Stark.

"There's three ways you can pull a gun," Stark told him without inflection. For all of them, you stand up straight. Only your arm and shoulder need to move."

"I'm listening," Ronnie said.

"First is the straight pull. Your hand takes the gun as it comes up." Stark demonstrated with a casual flex of his arm. He didn't make it particularly fast, but Ronnie's eyes widened a little. "Second, you can use your wrist to snap the gun up out of the holster. I've seen men try this way and end up throwing a gun across a room because they didn't have a decent grip." Stark's wrist made a sharp, jerking movement that brought the big Peacemaker up and leveled without the slightest of wobbles.

Ronnie nodded attentively.

"Finally, there's a circular draw. You hold your hand a little ways out in front of your gun, then use a circular motion to grab it and pull it clear. Your hand sweeps back, grasps the butt, pulls the pistol out, and thrusts it forward a little as it comes clear." Again the .45 flickered out. "None of these methods is reliable for a target much over fifty feet away." Stark reholstered the Colt.

"Which way is best?"

Stark gave a hitch to his shoulders. "Depends on the man and the circumstance. For most folks, unless they're planning on making a career out of gunwork, and putting in a lot of hours, and rubbing a lot of blisters in practice, the straight pull is the best. It's the most natural of the three. The other two take some getting used to.''

Stark fell silent. Ronnie waited to see if there was any more, but Stark just eyed him levelly. He wasn't prone to giving away tricks of his trade, but before this was over, his life just might depend on how well Ronnie could handle a gun. And how well he could take advice. Ronnie's life might depend on the same thing.

Ronnie drew his wiry body erect and deliberately tried to ignore Stark's presence. He let his arm hang straight by his side. He made a sudden snapping movement with his wrist, but didn't try to turn it into a draw. After a moment he swept his hand back then forward in a circular motion. Again, he didn't touch his gun. Thoughtfully he chewed on his lower lip.

At last he set his shoulders, shook his arm once, then let it hang at his side. With a slow, smooth movement—not trying to hurry it this time—he brought his hand up and pulled his gun clear of leather. Stark saw his legs tense as he resisted the natural urge to fall into a crouch. Ronnie brought the gun level. Its barrel held steady.

Still ignoring Stark, Ronnie repeated the movement again, and then again. Each time it was a little more natural. His body became more relaxed. At last he dropped the gun back into its holster and turned to Stark.

''Not bad,'' Stark allowed.

A brief grin of satisfaction tugged at Ronnie's mouth. ''I'll keep working on it,'' he vowed.

Stark wheeled away to see to the sorrel.

Remaining in the cool shade beside the creek was a temptation. Stark resisted it. The water was a magnet for riders, including Burke's men. Better for him and Ronnie to head on south a spell longer before they holed up to make plans.

"Dust over yonder," Ronnie spoke up once they'd put the creek about a mile behind them.

Stark followed the direction of his nod. Just as the mustanger had said, a faint haze of dust hung in the air several hills distant.

"Cattle," Ronnie surmised aloud. "A herd of them being driven from the south."

Stark agreed with him. "Let's go have a look-see."

Skirting the high ground, they worked their way toward the slowly moving dust cloud. Soon the bellowing and bawling of cattle on the move, along with the faint shouts of drovers, confirmed their guess.

"Pull up," Stark ordered. "They're just over this ridge. We'll hoof it from here."

Sprawled belly down in the grass atop the hogback, they peered through the thin dust haze at a herd of about two hundred head of cattle being hazed northward by a handful of riders. Stark used his field glasses to study the riders. They had the shiftless, hunted look of no-account wide-loopers. He spotted at least three different brands in the herd.

"Rustlers." Ronnie didn't need the evidence of a closer look to draw his conclusions. His voice was a growl. "Let's take them. Could be some stock belonging to Cass or Stu in that bunch!"

"Not so fast." Stark's firm grip halted his effort to retreat down the slope to their horses.

"But, darn it . . ."

"You didn't hire me to chase down two-bit rustlers," Stark reminded with only the barest glance over at him. "You hired me to bust up Burke's operation. It's pretty clear those yahoos are taking that herd to deliver to the compound. This could play right into our hands."

"Yeah? How you figure?"

Stark didn't answer right away. He mulled his notion over in detail. Below, the thirsty cattle had scented the creek and were pressing eagerly on toward it.

"Burke's stock pens are already full," Stark calculated aloud. "That means they'll have to pasture these outside."

A stray heifer broke from the herd and dashed toward the ridge where they lay concealed. One of the riders swung wide to cut her off. Stark's mouth thinned. He slid one hand down his leg to the butt of his .45, but didn't draw it. He glimpsed the sharp glance Ronnie gave him.

Both of them lay motionless as the owlhoot swerved his mount in front of the stray yearling at the very foot of the ridge. Stark could've cropped him with a single shot from his pistol. He made no move, and sensed Ronnie's bitter frustration.

With a hoarse yell the outlaw drover kept his horse at the heifer's heels until she once more joined the ranks of the herd.

Stark drew his hand away from his gun. He didn't speak again until the herd was well past their position.

Then he slipped down the slope a little ways and hinged himself to his feet. Ronnie joined him. The younger man's gaze was questioning.

''Come tonight, we'll head back to the hideout and try to give Tallant and his boys some religion.'' Stark didn't look at him as he answered his unspoken query.

''How we going to do that?''

Stark looked around at him and showed his teeth in a smile. ''We'll put the fear of the devil into them.''

Chapter Seven

"Rise and shine, mustanger; we got work to do," the laconic tones of Jim Stark came, rousing Ronnie Hall from a restless sleep.

The wrangler sat up groggily in his bedroll, peering at the tall, somehow sinister figure of Stark looming over him in the darkness. Seemingly satisfied he was awake, Stark wheeled away.

Ronnie scrambled to his feet and rolled up his bedding. Stark was already fooling with the horses. Ronnie had always figured himself to be a light sleeper, but apparently Stark had been up and about some little time without disturbing him. Ronnie shook his head. He couldn't recollect ever having met up with anyone quite like the Peacemaker.

Orphaned as a kid by one of the last Indian uprisings, Ronnie had made his way working with horses, first as a livery boy, then as a wrangler and bronc buster, and finally as a horse trader and breeder. From the meager beginnings of a single brood mare and a half-wild stallion he'd corralled himself, he had built up a string of horses and was getting a rep as a good man to do business with when it came to horseflesh.

All things considered, he was content with the small cabin, sturdy corral, and newly finished barn that were the main structures on his spread. With pastureland easy to lease from the tribes, he had just about all he needed.

The only thing lacking, he reckoned, was some sweet young gal who'd be willing to get hitched to a horse trader like himself, and make a real home out of his cabin. Ruefully, though, he had to admit the chances of finding a prize like that in the fastness of Indian Territory were mighty small indeed.

Shrugging such tomfoolery aside, he finished seeing to his bedding; then, with it tucked under his arm, he moved to where Stark was just tightening the cinch on the big sorrel he called Red. Fine-looking horse, Ronnie reflected, not for the first time. Plenty of bottom to him. Ronnie had always had a special touch with horses, but Stark was no tenderfoot in that respect himself. He seemed to know horses almost as well as he knew guns and fighting.

''Breakfast.'' Finished with the sorrel, Stark turned and shoved a couple of strips of jerky toward Ronnie. His tone was dry.

''Obliged.'' Ronnie stuck the strips in his shirt pocket and glanced up at the stars overhead in the night sky. Some past midnight, he calculated. To work, Stark's plan needed the cover of darkness. The troubleshooter had allowed them plenty of that.

Ronnie swigged water from his canteen, then saw to his own mount. The gray snorted its displeasure as he hefted the hull into place. Ronnie soothed the animal with a few soft words. With the saddle cinched, he pulled out one of the strips of jerky, broke off a piece, and began to chew on it. Knuckling his eyes, still encrusted from sleep, he crossed to where Stark knelt by the bed of their small fire from the night before.

Stark glanced around as he approached, then rose to his full imposing height. Ronnie saw that he'd been thrusting the blade of his heavy bowie knife into the dead ashes of the fire. The sheen of the twelve-inch blade was dulled by the coating of soot, he realized, so it would not cast a betraying gleam.

"Quite a pigsticker," he commented around the jerky. He'd been wanting a better look at the wicked blade, but hadn't found the occasion or the gumption to ask to see it. Hombres like Stark were touchy about the tools of their livelihood.

Stark hesitated, then passed the knife to him, hilt-first. Ronnie understood it was a concession Stark didn't often make. As he took the weapon he saw Stark's hand drop casually to the butt of his holstered Colt. A chill that had nothing to do with the coolness of the night touched Ronnie's nape. Stark didn't trust any man very far.

The heft of the bowie was heavy in his fist. This was no ordinary skinning or cutting knife. The bowie was meant for nothing so much as killing. He examined it as best he could in the dim light. Oddly, there was a thin inlay of some softer metal—maybe brass—along the rear half of the top of the blade.

He tapped it with his finger. "Never seen nothing like this before."

"Old knife-fighting trick," Stark said shortly. "You parry another man's knife with that inlay, and his blade cuts into it so it's trapped. Gives you an opening.''

Ronnie's testing thumb found notches in the brass that showed it had been used for just that purpose. He didn't need to ask what had become of an opponent who'd let his knife get thus trapped by Jim Stark.

He passed the weapon back to its owner. The blackened blade disappeared into its sheath. Ronnie checked his own sidearm and rifle before they rode out.

They traveled like wraiths across the darkened prairie. The only sounds were the whisper of their horses' hooves, and the inhalations of the animals' breathing. When they'd made camp, Stark had insisted that they oil all of their leather gear so there'd be no risk of the creak of a saddle giving them away to some sharp-eared sentry.

Ronnie could sense the coiled danger in the dark figure riding beside him. He himself felt a kind of spirited tension that shortened his breath and tightened his muscles. But there was a grim purposefulness to Stark, a readiness, even a willingness, to deal in death and violence. At the moment, the Peacemaker seemed like anything but an agent of peace.

Ronnie estimated they had covered some three miles when Stark abruptly reined up and lifted his hand. Ronnie pulled the gray to a halt. He started to ask a question, then thought better of it and kept silent. Stark was as alert as a wolf scenting its prey for the first time. Ronnie held his breath.

After a span of heartbeats he heard the muted sounds of horsemen approaching at a walk. He realized that he and Stark must've intercepted the route of one of the pairs of outriders patrolling this region.

Stark brought the sorrel around, giving Ronnie only a peremptory toss of his head by way of direction. Ronnie put the gray in behind the sorrel as Stark ascended a rugged bluff overlooking the trail the outriders seemed to be following.

Below the crest, Stark halted once more and slid from the saddle, motioning for Ronnie to follow suit. The wrangler did his best to dismount silently. He caught Stark's whisper as the taller man leaned close.

"Use your kerchief to muzzle that gray, then follow me up to the rim. Bring your repeater. Cover me if this doesn't work out, but only shoot as a last resort. I don't want any noise if at all possible." There was no slightest hint in his manner that he had any doubts about his ability to do whatever he planned. He was just taking precautions.

Stark catfooted away up the slope. Hurriedly Ronnie muzzled his horse so it couldn't whinny at the mounts of the approaching riders. Then, Winchester in hand, he legged it up the slope in Stark's wake.

He all but stumbled over Stark hunkered just below the crest of the bluff. Stark motioned him flat. He himself remained crouched. With a return of that faint chill, Ronnie saw that the darkened blade of the fighting bowie jutted from one big fist.

Ronnie heard the creak of saddle leather, the plod of hooves, the sound of a man spitting tobacco juice. He heard the sound of his own heartbeat. He was sweating in the cool air. Beside him, Stark was as motionless as a carven gargoyle on a church.

Some ten feet below them the shadowy shapes of two horsemen hove into view. Stark gave no warning. One moment he was a silent, unmoving form. The next instant he had launched himself out and down. Ronnie glimpsed the black silhouette of his plunging shape.

Both moccasined feet smashed full into the nearest rider. Ronnie knew from the solid thud of impact that they wouldn't need to worry about that owlhoot in any fighting that was still to come anytime soon, maybe ever.

The force of the collision slammed the hombre sideward off his horse and into his partner. Stark rode both men to the ground like an avenging fury as the startled horses bolted. Ronnie lurched to his knees, levering a shell into the Winchester. He could see only a tangled, heaving mass of shadows on the trail below. Abruptly an arm was drawn back, then thrust down. Ronnie glimpsed the unmistakable silhouette of the big bowie knife.

Then the figure of Jim Stark came erect in a catlike crouch. The two forms at his feet were motionless. Ronnie lowered his rifle. He realized his mouth was wide open, and he shut it. A brief sense of chagrin touched him. He'd offered to help the Peacemaker, but so far he seemed to be about as much use to Stark as a fifth leg on a bronc.

In moments Stark rejoined him on the ridge. ''Catch their horses while I see to the bodies,'' he ordered tersely. He didn't seem to be breathing much harder than usual.

The two mounts hadn't gone far. By the time

Ronnie had used the gray to herd them back, Stark had concealed what was left of the two outriders in a low gully.

"Hobble the horses behind the ridge," he directed in low tones. "I don't want them being found before daylight."

That task done, they rode on, more swiftly now. Their course took them in a wide arc around the outlaw fortress so they came down upon it from the north. They encountered no other guards, and when at last they gained a vantage point, there was little sign of life in the compound itself.

As Stark had foretold, the newly arrived cattle were pastured outside the wall. They were little more than a blacker mass on the darkened prairie. Stark took his time looking things over.

"Three drovers," he advised, and pointed them out.

Ronnie looked where he indicated, but couldn't make out much. Still, he wasn't prone to doubt Stark's word. He tried to memorize their positions.

"I'll swing off to the east," Stark went on. "When I signal, we start them moving. You keep on their tails and don't let them slow until they're good and scattered. I'll hang back a little ways and deal with the drovers."

"Right," Ronnie acknowledged. He was eager for action. Maybe he could earn his keep after all.

"Meet me back at the camp if we don't hook up before then," Stark said. *"Vaya con Dios."* Turning the sorrel, he loped away into the darkness.

* * *

For the first time Stark was pleased to have Ronnie along. Stampeding the herd while keeping watch for the drovers was a two-man job. The young bronc buster had already proved to have a fair amount of horse sense between his ears, and to be willing enough to follow orders. Stark was hoping he could avoid testing his nerve in a gun fracas, but he knew the likelihood of that was small. In fact, he admitted, Ronnie's mettle under fire just might be tried tonight.

The breeze felt good in Stark's face. He was glad to finally be locking horns with the enemy. Already on this outing he had thinned their ranks by two. And the number still could go higher.

He reined Red in and eased him up a low hill until he could peer over its crest. He had a clear view of the herd some fifty yards distant. The trio of gunmen doing duty as drovers were drifting along on the outer edges, well separated from another. After being driven up from the Indian Lands, the cattle were mostly quiet. Stark figured to change that.

He glanced one time toward the spot where Ronnie was supposed to be waiting. Then, sliding the shotgun from its sheath, he urged Red up to the top of the hill. He levered the shotgun, braced its butt at an angle against the saddle, then put heels hard to the sorrel and let loose a keening rebel yell. As the sorrel surged forward, Stark triggered the shotgun.

Its blast split the night with a cannon's roar and flame. Stark yelled again, tearing down on the startled herd like some ravening demon. Deftly he sheathed the shotgun, ripped his .38 from behind his back and emptied it into the night sky. He wanted the shotgun and the .45 held in reserve. He was dimly aware of other shots sounding somewhere off to his left accompanied by a yodeling howl. Ronnie had joined the action.

Bellows lifted from the herd to add to the racket. The cattle started to move, the back ranks lunging into those ahead until the whole mass was surging across the plains.

Close at their heels, Stark hoorawed them on. The racing herd gathered momentum. When he was sure they were moving into the wild run of a stampede, Stark drew up a trifle, swapping the .38 once more for the shotgun. The churning hooves had stirred the dust. Stark swung his head back and forth, squinting through the haze with narrowed eyes.

A centaur figure came tearing at him from the side, six-gun spitting lead. At least one of the drovers was more interested in downing him than halting the panicked cattle. Stark twisted in his saddle, letting the reins go briefly slack. Red never slowed. Stark snapped the shotgun to his shoulder and let fly. The recoil jarred him so he had to clamp his legs tight to stay mounted. At a range of thirty feet, the spreading buckshot tore the gunman from his saddle and made his horse squeal in pain and veer aside. Stark swept on past, levering the shotgun, searching for another target. The ranks of the enemy had just grown thinner still.

He angled along the rear of the racing herd. Ronnie's yells and the popping of his six-shooter reached him clearly above the thunder of hooves. He spotted another mounted form bearing toward Ronnie's position, and cut loose again with the shotgun. This time the load was a solid slug. It missed the drover, but came close enough to make him shear off and hightail it back toward the compound.

Stark couldn't account for the third drover, but the herd was well away from the outlaw fortress now, still being harried by Ronnie. Stark calculated the wrangler was clear of danger. He pulled Red to a halt and thumbed two loads of buckshot from his bandolier to replace the rounds he'd fired.

The herd was fading into the night. He stayed where he was, facing back toward the compound. Lights were flaring there, and within another couple of minutes he heard the yells and hoofbeats of riders coming hard after the cattle.

He judged their distance. He couldn't tell their number, but, as he'd planned, he was between them and the herd. When they were close enough he lifted the shotgun and levered and fired as fast as he could work the mechanism, sweeping the barrel in an arc. Three charges of buckshot and one solid load ripped the night. The muzzle blasts blinded him. Even over the ringing in his ears, he fancied he heard yells and cries of consternation. Immediately he spun Red and took off on a zigzag course. Looking back he saw the firefly sparks of gunfire, but none of the shots came near him.

He felt a hard, eager satisfaction. Tallant's minions wouldn't be too quick to come after them tonight. Tomorrow, Stark was willing to let them come.

Chapter Eight

Tallant had sent his men out in groups of three to try to retrieve the stampeded herd. In the morning sunlight, Stark and Ronnie watched one such trio from the shadow of a nearby ridge. A few hours of sleep had been all that Stark had allowed them.

He had known roughly how Tallant would react to the raid. With a newly arrived herd of rustled cattle scattered from here to gone, Tallant had been forced to take action. He couldn't afford to let that many cattle be lost. So he had sent his gunsels out to do their best to round them up. And he had done it in threes for protection.

Tallant knew now that he was being harassed by a dangerous and elusive foe. Even if he handn't yet found the bodies of his outriders, the raid on the cattle would've convinced him that he faced more than just the rustling of some already stolen beeves. Tallant's men would be on the alert, but they would also be unhappy at having to spend their time rounding up cattle. No doubt there were a few genuine cowpunchers among the crew, but this trio had the look of hardcases.

Stark was conscious of Ronnie's expectant presence beside him. The mustanger had acquitted himself well

75

last night, and this morning he looked chipper and ready for more action.

Stark pulled the shotgun from its scabbard and, without taking his gaze off the hardcase threesome, switched the solid loads in its magazine for buckshot. Deliberately he levered a shell softly into the chamber and left the gun on full cock.

"Back my play," he said then.

Ronnie's eyes widened. "What are you figuring to do?"

"Give those boys out there a chance to repent," Stark told him, and gigged the sorrel into the open.

One of the trio saw him almost instantly. They were alert, all right. They watched him come with cold, wary eyes, their hands hovering near their weapons. Stark rode with the barrel of the shotgun pointed skyward, and since he looked to offer no immediate threat, no hand was raised against him.

Stark sized them up as he drew near. They were of the same dangerous breed that had been backing Tallant in Sod Town. The one to his right looked grubby and mean. A wide mustache curled above thin lips. As Stark approached, the fellow casually slid his Winchester repeater from its sheath and held it in the same position as Stark carried the shotgun. So he favored a long gun, Stark assessed.

The middle rider was short and squint-eyed. Stark felt a tingle of concern as he saw the Greener sawed-off double-barrel shotgun canted across the small man's saddle. He himself wasn't the only gunman in these parts who favored a shotgun, Stark mused darkly. The Greener looked too big for its owner, but he doubted that was the case.

The third hombre packed twin six-guns, holstered for a cross draw. He seemed content to lean his folded arms on his saddle horn and sneer at Stark from a face that was mostly mouth and nose. In that position he was all set to make his draw.

Stark began to question if he'd bitten off more than he could chew. Bracing three gunslicks like these might be a greenhorn's play. It might be his last play. He wondered how their horses would react if it came to gunwork. Firing a gun from a spooked bronc was one thing; hitting a target was another.

Stark pulled Red up some twelve feet in front of the trio. They could've shifted farther apart to make it harder for one man to go against them, but they were too confident in their numbers to take that precaution. Their mistake, Stark thought. He hoped it made a difference.

"Morning, gents," he greeted laconically.

"Who are the deuce are you?" the little one with the shotgun demanded in surly tones.

"Just a man with some advice," Stark told him.

"Yeah? And what might that be?"

Stark smiled coldly. "Shuck your guns and ride out of here, and I'll let you live."

The spokesman gave a snort of surprise. They all gaped at Stark.

"Say what?" the mustached yahoo drawled.

"You heard me. I don't cotton to bushwhacking you, so I'm giving you a chance to cut loose from

Tallant on your own. Otherwise, I'll cut you loose my-self.''

They were too tough to be much impressed. ''What's your handle, stranger?'' the shotgun man snapped.

''James Stark.''

Now they were impressed, but, Stark saw, it wasn't going to help. He knew which way this was going to break. Sometimes, like with the pard of the ambitious Stace back in Guthrie, Stark's name and the rep he carried could buy him free of trouble. But this time it wasn't going to buy him anything except a moment's stunned hesitation.

He used it for all it was worth. Even before their gun hands started to move, Stark pounded his heels into Red and sent the big sorrel plunging forward. In the same instant he dropped the shotgun level and pulled the trigger.

The twin barrels of the small man's Greener were swinging toward him; the two-gun hombre's hands were snatching his irons clear of leather; the rifle toter was jacking a shell into place, when the charge of .00 buckshot tore into their ranks.

The Greener blasted to one side as its owner was flung backward by the brunt of the charge. In that very moment Red slammed into his smaller horse and spun the beast aside. The rifleman's mount spooked as if a burr had been shoved under its saddle. A six-gun cracked to Stark's left, and hot lead burned through the air near his ear.

Stark hauled Red hard around. The two-gun shootist and his horse had caught some buckshot, whether from the lever-action or his own compadre's Greener, Stark didn't know. His wounded horse was panicked, but the rider wasn't finished. As he fought to control the animal, he threw lead with a single remaining pistol. His aim was wild, and Stark had his chance to get the shotgun pointed generally in his direction and unleash another load of double ought. That finished him. The shootist flew from the saddle in a wild flail of arms, his second gun spinning away.

And then there was only the rifleman to worry about. Stark wheeled Red again. If not for the rifleman's spooked bronc, Stark knew the hardcase would've already finished him. But his own big sorrel, Red, had been trained not to lose his head under gunfire, and maybe, against the rifleman, that had just saved Stark's life. The hardcase had been too occupied with calming his mount to get off a shot.

He was just getting the beast back under his command as Stark wheeled toward him. One-handed, he tried to lever the Winchester with a snap of his arm. Stark knew he had him; knew he had plenty of time to line the shotgun again.

He never needed to pull the trigger. From the nearby ridge came a whipcrack of sound, and the rifleman spilled from his horse, which went off into yet another bucking spree. Stark's head turned sharply. Ronnie was lowering his rifle. Stark had all but forgotten the wrangler's presence.

Shotgun still at ready, Stark guided Red past each of the fallen gunsels. There were no signs of life. He glanced about as Ronnie came cantering up on the gray. The younger man's eyes were wide. He halted and stared down at the body of the rifleman.

"Nice shot," Stark allowed.

Ronnie pulled his gaze away from his victim. "You would've got him," he said with something like awe. "You didn't need me to drop him."

"You never know for certain in a gunfight," Stark told him. "And it doesn't hurt to have a good man backing your play."

Ronnie blinked at the offhanded compliment, then shook his head in amazement. "It was so blamed fast. I dismounted, and then everything was almost over before I even got my rifle raised."

Starked studied the surrounding countryside. The brief gun battle didn't seem to have drawn any immediate attention, but he doubted it would be long before more of Tallant's riders were headed their way.

"Do we hide the bodies?" Ronnie had recovered enough to ask hoarsely. The prospect clearly wasn't appealing to him.

"Nope. This time we want them to be found."

Ronnie didn't try to hide his relief. "So, what's next?"

"We let Tallant's boys start to sweat while we head back to Sod Town and try to scare up a decent meal. Then we find a safe campsite and take it easy. Come mañana, we'll have a few more surprises for Tallant."

Ronnie started to chuckle and then laugh. "If that don't beat all! We're chowing down in town while Tallant's out here beating the bushes for us!"

Stark reloaded the shotgun. "He won't have to beat them very far if we don't get riding."

They kept to cover as they headed for Sod Town. Stark took them across stretches of barren terrain that would leave no sign of their passage. Once he spotted a lone horseman whipping his steed hard toward the south. He put his field glasses on the rider and thought he recognized him as one of the gunslingers who'd been with Tallant in the saloon. The range was long for a rifle shot, and, for all he knew, the gunsharp might be deserting Tallant's ranks. With a shrug, Stark lowered the glasses.

Although they approached the town carefully, there was no sign of Tallant or his hardcases in the community. The gun boss was closing ranks. When he found the trio of gunmen, two of them dead by shotgun blasts, he would know for certain who he was up against. Right now, Sod Town was likely the safest place for them to be.

They scrounged an edible meal at the dirt-walled café under the worried eye of the proprietor. Word of their presence would reach Tallant not long after they rode out, Stark calculated.

They left town unmolested. Midafternoon found them in a remote draw, the rim of which offered a commanding view of the range. Taking watches in shifts, they dozed while the horses grazed. Stark judged it safe enough to remain there for the night.

They were on the move in the small hours of morning long before the sun was up. The prairie was pale and ghostly in the moonlight reflected from a distant bank of clouds. Lightning flickered there, and, seconds later, the far-off rumble of thunder rolled faintly to them. An early fall thunder boomer was sweeping across the grasslands, but they were well clear of its path.

As Stark was hoping, Tallant had pulled his outriders closer to the headquarters. Riders in pairs or trios had proven themselves too vulnerable. Tallant wasn't looking to lose any more men if he could help it. That made Stark's plan easier to carry out.

He found a secluded niche in an outcropping of sandstone and installed Ronnie there. "Be ready to start taking shots at the compound with your Winchester," he told the younger man.

Ronnie squinted into the darkness. "Too far for my rifle," he objected.

"Maybe for yours," Stark returned, "But not for this one." He slapped the butt of the Sporting Rifle in its sheath. "You let me worry about hitting anything; I just want you to keep them thinking there are two sharpshooters targeting them."

"Where will you be?"

Stark waved an arm in the direction of the rustlers' fortress. "Over yonder on the other side. We'll be out of range of most of what they can throw at us. So long as you keep your head down, you should be safe enough. If they come after you, just pull out and we'll hook up later. But I think they'll be too busy ducking to mount any sort of sally. Ride out three hours after daylight unless you hear different."

He added a few other instructions, then rode off. By first light he was safely hidden overlooking the compound at a range of just under a thousand yards. He had a scope sight in place on the Sporting Rifle.

Outfitted with a custom barrel, the 1886 rifle was

nothing so much as a repeating buffalo gun, with a range and caliber to match the Big Fifty Sharps favored by the buffalo hunters of old. But whereas the Sharps was a single-shot weapon, the Sporting Rifle's magazine held eight rounds. Stark had acquired the piece after a recent dissatisfying experience with a Sharps he'd appropriated from a would-be drygulcher. He still favored the shotgun, with its shorter length, for most fighting requiring a long gun. But for distance work, the Sporting Rifle, he was convinced, had no peer.

As daylight grew, he sighted in on the compound. Through the scope he saw the young blond woman he'd noticed before emerge from Tallant's cabin and move with dragging steps and bowed head toward the mess hall. Maybe that explained why none of the gunsels laid a hand on her. She belonged to Tallant. From what he could see of her face, she was pretty, but her gait and the sag of her shoulders bespoke a physical and spiritual exhaustion.

Stark lifted his head and frowned before pressing his eye back to the scope.

Tallant's hirelings were stirring. Stark was amused to note that less than half of the stampeded herd had been rounded up. He focused on the watchtower. The lookout seemed intent on scanning the countryside opposite Stark's position, where Ronnie was concealed. Stark tried to spot the wrangler himself, but, even knowing Ronnie's approximate location, he had no luck. He hoped the outlaw lookout didn't do any better from his nearer vantage point.

Stark's location was well shaded, so he had no concern that reflection would reveal his presence. He continued his leisurely survey of the compound until the morning chores were under way. A few loafers were awaiting breakfast, and the night outriders had returned from duty to be replaced by new pairs of horsemen. Tallant himself was striding about angrily issuing orders and glaring occasionally out at the prairie.

When it looked as though the gun boss was organizing a group of men to mount some sort of search or patrol, Stark decided he'd waited long enough.

He swung the scope back to the lookout in the watchtower. He didn't like killing this way, but he couldn't afford to have the tower manned. And, given the chance, he figured the yahoo stationed there would gun him down in cold blood without a spark of remorse. At least, Stark reflected bitterly, he had his share of remorse for what he was about to do, necessary though it was.

He tested the slight breeze, compensated for the drop of the bullet in flight, then, lying flat, snugged the brass-shod butt against his shoulder. The smooth wood felt warm where his cheek pressed against it. Deliberately he squeezed the trigger.

The report was like a clap of thunder right overhead. He felt the recoil all the way to the soles of his feet. He pressed his eye once more to the sight in time to see the tiny figure of the lookout stagger back a step and topple from the tower.

The sound of the shot would only now be reaching the fortress, Stark calculated as he shifted his aim immediately to the spot where he'd last seen Tallant.

Pick off the gun boss, and he might've gone a long way toward shutting down the whole operation. But he got only a glimpse of Tallant's rawboned form diving for the cover of a shed. Faster than any of his men, the gun boss had realized what had happened and sought shelter.

His mouth tight with anger at the man's escape, Stark picked the fellow who'd been standing nearest Tallant. That worthy had frozen. The big shell from the Sporting Rifle smashed him off his feet before he had time to move.

Men and horses were starting to react now. Old hands for the most part, the hired guns knew when to take cover. A few threw wild shots. Stark clipped a third one who made a dash for the vacant tower.

He kept firing, working the lever and pumping shells down into the midst of the camp. He scored no more hits as his targets scrambled for cover.

The magazine ran dry. Stark shifted positions, reloading by feel as he moved, his eyes intent on the compound. Distantly came the crack of a Winchester. Ronnie was doing his part. To the startled outlaws it would seem that a pair of sharpshooters had bracketed the fortress.

A few of them were throwing lead back, but the range was too great for them to be effective. And with his change of location, they had no real idea of where Stark was. All three of his victims lay in motionless, broken sprawls. Following Stark's lead, Ronnie's firing tapered to a halt.

Stark waited patiently. He saw flickers of movement—men testing to see if he was still out there.

Maybe they were acting on Tallant's orders, or, could be, some were acting on their own initiative. No professional liked to be pinned down like a tenderfoot. The sounds of shouted voices drifted up to him, although he couldn't make out the words.

Tallant, along with several other men, Stark thought, had ended up in the stable. He kept a lot of his attention there. It was hard to watch everywhere at once.

Suddenly gunfire erupted from a half-dozen points. He saw the smoke before he heard the shots. He couldn't tell where any of the bullets went. The guns were mostly rifles, but their range still fell far short of his position.

Stark scowled. He'd hoped to lure some more of them into the open, but Tallant looked to be too smart to let that happen. He'd already lost three men to the sniping. Also, judging from the return fire, it seemed that the gun boss had figured out that the real danger lay with Stark. Ronnie was being pretty much ignored.

Spitefully Stark put a careful shot at each one of the points of return fire. He didn't know if he'd done any damage, but two of the rifles fell silent.

He switched to yet a different vantage point and emptied another magazine methodically into the stable. Even at this range the Sporting Rifle might well punch a hole through a board wall and into a hiding gunman. The horses, if any were in there, would just have to take their chances.

Stark stopped firing and reloaded thoughtfully, looking about for a new position. With no warning, something like a large metal wasp kicked up a fistful of dirt maybe a yard below him. A low boom came rumbling faintly after.

Stark wriggled backward. Some sorry beggar down there had a long-range, heavy-caliber rifle of his own, and he knew how to use it. The big slug had come deuced close, and Stark wasn't sure just where the shooter was located.

He might've played this hand as far as he could, he reflected gloomily. Plainly Tallant's men were managing to change positions without being spotted. But it rankled to be run off before he was good and ready to leave.

He sent a random shot into the compound. A fusillade of small arms fire responded. Mingled with it came the heavier report of the sharpshooter's rifle. At one-second intervals, three big slugs tore the soil near him. A Sharps, Stark concluded with certainty. And its owner could reload with speed only an expert could manage.

And Stark had him spotted at last.

The marksman was shooting from a tiny shed at the edge of the encampment. It gave him a good field of fire, but it also made it impossible for him to do much in the way of shifting positions after he fired. In short, it made him almost a sitting target.

On his belly, Stark snaked a dozen feet through the buffalo grass until he could peer down at the fortress from a slightly different angle. Telltale traces of smoke still hung in front of the shed, although the sharpshooter could not be seen.

Coolly Stark sighted in on the small structure. Occasional gunfire came from other points of the compound. Far off, Ronnie was firing futilely. Stark ignored it all. With calm deliberation, taking a heartbeat to aim after each shot, he poked a straight line of eight holes through the board wall of the shed. The last empty cartridge slipped out of the breech as he levered it clear. The other shooting had stopped. Stark squinted through the scope at his target.

The door jerked as if something had hit it from within. It swung open a span of inches and the familiar lethal shape of a Big Fifty toppled out into the dust. There was no further movement from inside the shack. Stark thumbed one more shell into the Sporting Rifle, sighted carefully, and smashed the mechanism of the Sharps into scrap metal. Nobody else among Tallant's crew would be using that particular weapon against him.

He'd definitely been there long enough, Stark decided. He was pushing his luck. There were outriders to be concerned about, and Tallant might well have access to other marksmen with sharpshooter rifles. Stark worked his way back from his latest vantage point and returned to Red.

Mounted, he headed at a fast clip for the spot where he'd left Ronnie. There was still a good span of time before the allotted period was up. He hoped the wrangler would realize that he was no longer firing, and follow suit himself.

He reined the sorrel sharply into a draw as the nearing pound of hoofbeats warned him. A pair of outriders tore recklessly past, headed in the general direction of the ridge he had just departed. Stark fingered the shotgun but let them go. He heeled Red into motion again.

He had reached the higher country on the opposite side of the compound when he pulled up so hard that Red snorted his displeasure. Stark whipped his field glasses to his eyes, lining them on the handful of horsemen descending to the encampment.

"Blast!" he gritted aloud.

Straddling his gray, hands bound behind him, the wiry form of Ronnie Hall was plainly visible in the midst of the quartet of mounted hardcases escorting him as their prisoner down to the gates of the fortress.

Stark half drew the Sporting Rifle from its sheath, then stopped, his jaw working angrily. He couldn't fire without the risk of hitting Ronnie, and if he did renew his sniping attack, then he had no doubt Ronnie would suffer the consequences, most likely with his life. As it stood, Ronnie would have it rough enough without adding fuel to the flames. Reluctantly he slid the rifle back into the scabbard.

He didn't know what had gone wrong. Maybe Tallant had sent out a night patrol, suspecting that Stark might be planning to slip up on the camp under cover of darkness. Unknowingly he and Ronnie had evaded them, but, returning to the fold with morning light, they had happened upon the mustanger and taken him prisoner.

But it didn't really matter what had happened. Tallant had turned the tables on him. Now Ronnie was his hostage, and Stark's hands were tied just as tightly as those of the captive wrangler.

Chapter Nine

"Members of the jury, the law is clear," Prudence McKay declared. "I have recounted the facts to you. Those also are clear. Even the Old Testament recognizes the right of a man to act in self-defense. My client was faced with a man who could and would kill him if he did not act first. He did so, thereby saving his life, but only by a bare second's time. If he had not drawn first, then his opponent—an infamous gunman as you have heard—would most certainly have taken his life."

She paused to draw breath, trying to read the effect of her words on the jury. Across the crowded courtroom, she knew U.S. prosecutor Damon Rasters would be smirking confidently at her. In pursuing his cases, the ambitious young prosecutor was as savage and relentless as the weasel she unkindly thought him to resemble.

And he was not without some reason for confidence. Her client, one Hal Sweet, had something of a reputation himself as a rowdy and a troublemaker, but not as a gunfighter. However, in the skilled hands of Rasters, eager as he was for a murder conviction to further his own reputation, Sweet had come across looking like a desperado every bit as despicable and violent as the notorious gunman he'd managed to kill.

There was no question, either, that there had been good reason for Sweet to fear for his life. His victim, Dude Wilkin, had come looking for him upon learning that Sweet had been secretly romancing Wilkin's girl. He had vowed before witnesses to kill Sweet. But there had been no standup gunfight. Catching sight of his nemesis first, Sweet, fully aware of the threats, had yelled a challenge, then pulled his revolver and emptied it at that worthy before Wilkin had had a fair chance to draw his own gun.

Cold-blooded murder, or self-defense?

Eyeing the stolid faces of the jurors, Prudence knew she needed something more to sway them to her client's side, to make them understand that, sometimes, when the prize was great, you couldn't afford to give the enemy an even chance, because to do so was to lose the prize.

Then, with a shudder, she realized what she had to do to win her case.

"I killed a man once," she announced flatly, and saw by their startled reactions that she had succeeded, at least, in getting the jurors' attention.

She was conscious of the presence of Rasters, of the anxious face of her towheaded, weak-jawed client, of the sharp attention of the white-haired judge, and of the heat in the courtroom. But it wasn't the heat alone that was making her perspire beneath the dark, high-necked dress she customarily wore in court. She hoped she still looked reasonably presentable as she offered her closing argument.

"It happened when I had been kidnapped by Dirk Garland and his gang," she went on with her narrative. Her voice tightened with emotion that, although theatrical, was nevertheless very real. "I was cornered by one of the outlaws. James Stark, known as the Peacemaker, had given me a pistol so I could defend myself. He was the man who ultimately rescued me, but he was nowhere near when I was confronted by this brigand."

A natural orator, she had to do little to add to the drama of the tale as she spun it. The jury, indeed, the entire courtroom, she sensed, was listening raptly to her account.

"It was James Stark himself who had, shortly before, taught me—no, showed me—that when the odds are against you, sometimes giving your enemy a chance is the same thing as surrender and defeat. I could not surrender to this outlaw." She left unsaid what her surrender would've meant, although she was certain the fierce blush she felt rising to her face would tell them all they needed to know.

"I shot him," she finished simply. "I shot him because I had no choice. Later, that killing was ruled self-defense." She drew a deep breath. "Members of the jury, before you convict Hal Sweet of murder, place yourself in his position, or your daughter in mine, and ask yourself what choice either of us really had."

She took her seat in silence, fighting to hold back tears that were every bit as real as the emotions her narrative had awakened in her. Her client stared at her with wide eyes. She only dimly heard the judge's instructions, although she had regained her composure, and rose to her feet as the jury filed out and Sweet was escorted back to jail. She busied herself collecting her papers.

"Congratulations, Counselor." The sneer that had been on the face of Damon Rasters had carried over to his voice. "Now, in order to convict your wretched client, they'll have to also convict you, and their own daughters."

Prudence faced the spiteful prosecutor across the counsel table. "They haven't given their verdict yet," she reminded demurely.

"But you know as well as I do how they'll decide." The prosecutor's anger at his impending loss gave an acid bite to his words. "I'm surprised that you would stoop to such cheap theatrical tactics."

"This was a case that should never have been brought," Prudence retorted coldly. "Those charges shouldn't even have been filed. You're just cluttering up the court's docket for your own political ends."

Rasters reddened. "Nonsense! Your client is a ruffian and a troublemaker—"

"Then charge him with that," Prudence cut him off, "or with manslaughter. Don't charge him with murder!"

Rasters stalked away. Prudence finished organizing her papers. The courtroom had emptied. She questioned to herself how long the jury would be out. Did she have time to run over to her office and clear a few things off her desk?

Tired suddenly, she opted to simply sit back down at the table and pensively contemplate the courtroom. She had deliberately used Jim Stark's name, knowing it would evoke a favorable reaction from the jury. Jim was well thought of by most law-abiding folks in the area. And it had been his own advice to her that had given her the idea for the argument she'd employed.

That was two more debts she owed him, she supposed. The thought only made the irritation she'd been cultivating for him that much harder to maintain. Where was the man, for heaven's sake? Where had he gone without so much as a by-your-leave? Had he forgotten his commitment to serve as an expert witness?

A little aggravating voice somewhere in her mind pointed out that she was getting entirely too worked up over the unexplained, and no doubt temporary, absence of a witness. The trial date hadn't even been set yet. Honest by nature, she tried never to fool herself. Curbing her errant emotions, she sought to analyze the situation with the same careful objectivity she applied to her legal cases.

She wasn't sure she succeeded. It was foolish to deny that her feelings toward Jim Stark had changed since she'd first met him a few months before. From seeing him as a ruthless, though undeniably attractive, hired killer, she had come to know him as a charming, thoroughly masculine man of deep moral convictions and fiber. She still got giddy thinking of how it had felt to be swirled about the dance floor in his arms.

But over and above it all, he remained a man whose life was devoted to violence, albeit on the side of right and justice. Such a man could never hold a significant place in her heart.

In fact, for every good quality she could list in him, some other equally unappealing quality could be found, she was certain. For instance, why had he run off without telling her? Undoubtedly it had to do with business, she reasoned coldly, which made it just that much worse. Why, he could be lying somewhere now out in the wilderness dead or wounded, with no one, including herself, the wiser. It was insufferable!

"Miss McKay. Prudence. Your office said you would be here. I'm glad I caught you. I have a matter we need to discuss." The familiar tones of Randall Burke brought her out of her reverie.

The restaurant owner advanced into the courtroom. He was smooth and urbane as always, but his manner carried none of the usual flirtatious airs he affected in her presence. His well-hewn features were set and serious.

Prudence rose. With an effort she set her personal affairs aside. "What is it, Randall?" She used his first name to put him at ease. "Do we need to go to my office to discuss it?" She was almost relieved to have a client's problems to address rather than her own.

Burke glanced about the empty courtroom. Plainly he did not want to postpone the discussion. "No, this is fine," he decided aloud and pulled out one of the chairs at the counsel table so he could face her when he sat. She saw he was freshly shaved, barbered, and powdered. For some reason it was slightly repellent.

She matched his concerned look with one of her own. She wasn't putting on an act. Her clients' problems did concern her. And Randall Burke was a good client, although she had done little for him since helping him establish his business when he'd come to Guthrie a bit over a year before. Nor had she responded to his romantic advances, although she was not certain why. He was a gentleman, and attractive enough, she supposed. However, she didn't approve of the gambling house he operated. It had not been a part of his operation when she'd handled the legal end of opening his restaurant. At any rate, her career left her little time for romantic interludes, particularly with former or potential clients.

"This is about your friend, James Stark," Burke advised bluntly.

Prudence felt her interest quicken. She couldn't seem to get away from matters having to do with Jim Stark. She sensed Burke's perceptive gaze on her. "He's more of an acquaintance than a friend," she heard herself correct him blandly, and knew an immediate twinge of guilt at the words. "I've represented him on one occasion," she added.

She couldn't tell if her denial pleased or displeased Burke. "Well, maybe you can help me get to the bottom of this," he went on.

"Get to the bottom of what?" Prudence was genuinely puzzled.

Burke drew a deep breath, making his broad shoulders strain the fabric of his tailored coat. "I've received disturbing news that the Peacemaker is interfering in my affairs." He made the sobriquet almost an insult.

"Interfering how?" For some reason, Prudence's heart speeded up as she asked the question.

Burke appeared to catch himself on the verge of saying something more. Instead he started over, though his voice was still tight. "Perhaps I'd better explain. I operate a cattle brokerage business in the

Unassigned Lands. I deliver cattle and horses from the small ranchers in the Indian Lands to the markets in Kansas.'' There was some kind of wariness in his eyes that made no sense to her.

''Go on,'' she urged. What was Jim Stark up to now? she asked herself.

''I just got a telegram from my range boss there. He sent a rider to the nearest telegraph station. He informs me that someone—he believes it to be Stark— is interfering violently with my operation.

''What do you mean?''

''I mean gunplay and bloodshed. Bushwhacking and guerrilla tactics used on my men!''

''Why would Mr. Stark do that?'' Prudence asked with real surprise.

''My guess is someone hired him. One of my business enemies perhaps. Stark is nothing more than a high-priced hired gun. Isn't that correct?''

''Well, yes, in a way, I suppose. But he's very careful to operate within the law.''

''There is no law in the Unassigned Lands,'' Burke said flatly. ''You're a lawyer; you know that.''

''Still, I don't think Mr. Stark would engage in such activities, even if someone offered to pay him to do so.'' A disquieting notion sparked suddenly in Prudence's mind. ''Are you sure your foreman is correct?'' she asked to cover whatever might show on her face.

''I'm sure,'' Burke said with conviction. ''It's Stark, all right. And if he's not doing it for money, then it occurred to me that there just might be another reason.''

Prudence's throat closed up tight. She inclined her head to indicate he should continue.

For the first time Burke showed some reluctance. But it was almost like an act. "I thought," he said hesitantly, "that the reasons might be, perhaps, personal in nature."

Prudence's racing heart faltered. Quite accurately Burke had hit on the disturbing idea that fluttered unpleasantly in her mind. "I don't understand," she said to buy time. It wasn't the truth. She understood all too well what he meant.

"I thought Stark might harbor hard feelings because I happened to pay some attention to you when you were in his company. Then, too, he lost a wager to me the very next night."

"A wager?" She'd never considered gambling as one of Stark's vices.

"Yes," Burke explained smoothly. "A contest of skill between Stark and my man Chin. Stark lost the bet. There was a roomful of witnesses. That, coupled with my attentions to you, might've provoked Stark into disrupting my business affairs."

"I'm sure Mr. Stark wouldn't do anything like that," Prudence heard herself restating her earlier protestations.

But was she sure? Was it possible Jim Stark was jealous over her favors? The personal ramifications of such a thing were more than she cared to contemplate. But, postponing that aspect of the matter, Jim had certainly reacted swiftly and with displeasure to Burke's intrusion at their dinner. And then, apparently, he had been humiliated by Burke's servant, before disappearing in a mysterious fashion.

How well did she know Jim Stark? Certainly not well enough to pretend to fully understand him. As she had just reflected, he was a man of violence. It was his chosen profession. And she had firsthand cause to know just how effective he was in that profession. Would he choose violent tactics to get even for the kind of slights he'd suffered at Burke's hands?

Prudence didn't believe he would, but, she confessed reluctantly to herself, she didn't quite disbelieve it either.

"I've already told you that I'm sure you're mistaken," she said with conviction that pleased her. "And I'm not sure why you've come to me with your suspicions. I haven't even seen Mr. Stark for well over a week."

"I came to you for two reasons. First, I'm going to put a halt to Stark's interference in my affairs." For a moment the coldness in his tone reminded Prudence of a similar iciness she'd had occasion to hear in Stark's voice. "If you can assist me, either personally or professionally, then I would certainly be appreciative. If there is legal action that can be taken, I would certainly want you to represent me."

The notion of bringing any sort of lawsuit against Jim was appalling. But, Prudence vowed to herself, she definitely intended to get to the bottom of this the next time she saw him.

"I have no influence on what Mr. Stark does or doesn't do," she stated coolly. "As for the legal end, that is something you should take up with the U.S. Marshal's Office, or that of the federal prosecutor.''

''They have no jurisdiction in the Unassigned Lands.'' Burke repeated his earlier legitimate objection. ''But at least I know now that I'll have to handle Stark in some other fashion.'' He gave a smile with neither warmth nor humor in it, and which sent a tremor of concern for Jim down her spine.

Then his sensual mouth grew fuller, and he looked at her in a way that made her shift uncomfortably. ''As for my second reason,'' he continued suavely, ''I wanted to assure myself that there was nothing of a personal nature between you and Mr. Stark. I take that to be the case?''

Trapped, Prudence thought. ''My personal affairs are my private business,'' she parried.

Burke actually seemed pleased. ''Of course; I understand. That's exactly as it should be. The relationship between two individuals should remain personal and . . . private. Don't you agree?''

Prudence didn't like the implications he somehow put in his words. The man would've made a good lawyer, she conceded wryly. ''That's quite correct,'' she assured him stiffly. ''Now, I really do have to prepare for the jury verdict.'' She made to rise.

Burke stood at the same moment, as though he'd planned it, and for a moment she was closer to him than she had any desire to be. She caught the sickly sweet scent of bay rum from him.

Then he stepped smoothly clear. ''My apologies for the intrusion.'' His smile was all oily warmth and charm. ''We can continue our discussion of personal matters another time. Good day, Prudence.''

She remained standing as he left the courtroom. Her legs felt a little weak, but she wouldn't allow herself the luxury of sinking back into the chair.

Her emotions were all atumble. She would deal with Randall Burke and his suddenly unwanted attentions when it became necessary. And she was worried about what plans he had for Jim. But for now her overriding desire was to confront Jim Stark and discover just what type of dangerous game he was playing, and what role, if any, she had in it.

Chapter Ten

Ronnie Hall awoke to darkness and immediately felt the aches and pains of the beating he'd taken. Nothing serious, he reminded himself; no worse than being thrown by a rowdy bronc. In the past, he'd taken a lot worse punishment from horses than Tallant and his men had dished out in trying to get him to tell what he knew about Jim Stark. He hadn't even had to lie when he answered them. He hadn't the foggiest idea where the Peacemaker was, or what he would do next now that he, Ronnie, had been fool enough to let himself get captured.

They'd come on him from behind, drawn by the sounds of his shooting—the same sounds that had deafened him to their approach. They'd had him under the barrels of four rifles before he knew they were there. He was used to sneaking up on horses, not to watching out for men sneaking up on him. Jim Stark, he suspected, wouldn't have been caught quite so flat-footed. But caught he himself had been, and there'd been nothing for it but to shuck his rifle and raise his hands.

His captors, he gathered, had been sent out by Tallant to prowl the vicinity of the compound during the night in hopes of intercepting Stark. They sure hadn't succeeded in doing that, he'd mused with grim satisfaction when they'd brought him into the fortress. Stark's long-range target practice had taken its toll both in lives and nerves. Even after the sniping stopped, it was near noon before Tallant's gunsels were willing to stay in the open for longer than a few moments at a time. And the riders Tallant had sent on patrol hadn't been any too eager to leave the protection of the compound. Stark had been earning his pay, all right. But, Ronnie acknowledged bitterly, his own carelessness had just made Stark's job a whole lot harder.

Achingly he sat up in the bunk and swung his booted feet to the floor as softly as he could. The shed was dark; it was night outside.

What had awakened him? Some noise, he thought.

He'd been in the shed since they'd gotten tired of questioning him and thumping on him that afternoon. He had a nasty hunch that more of the same, and likely a lot worse, was in store for him.

His prison had pretty clearly served that purpose for others before he'd taken up lodging here. It was well suited for use as a hoosegow.

The walls and floor were of railroad ties, and there were no windows, save a small one, high up, that wasn't large enough to let a man squeeze through. By its light he had examined the interior before the sun had gone down. What he'd found hadn't been encouraging. There was no breaching of those solid walls, even if he'd had a tool to do so. The door was made of thick planks banded with iron. It was barred from the outside and fit solidly enough in its frame so that there was no way to manipulate the bar from within.

What other prisoners had been held here? Ronnie wondered. And for what purpose? He didn't have many doubts of their final fate. No guard was posted. None was needed.

The noise came again, starting the blood pumping in him and clearing his head abruptly. It seemed to be coming from the door, as if someone was stealthily trying to shift the heavy bar securing it.

Heart pounding, Ronnie rose from the bunk and moved on his toes across the small room. The floor was solid enough so no creaking board betrayed him. He wished for a weapon, but there was nothing to serve. His gun belt had been taken from him. He got behind the door, far enough to one side so it wouldn't bump him if it was pushed all the way open. Clenching and unclenching his fists, he waited.

A muffled thud sounded from without. Whoever was fooling with the bar had gotten it loose, then dropped it. After a moment the door began to edge inward. It opened only far enough for a slender figure to slip into the cell.

Ronnie lunged, just as a tentative voice whispered, ''Can you hear me?''

It was too late to stop. Even if the voice hadn't warned him, Ronnie's grappling hands told him that form he'd attacked was definitely female.

He let go instantly as she managed to smother a startled cry. His hands felt like they were on fire.

''Shh! Be quiet!'' Her frantic whispered order silenced any outburst he might've made.

His visitor turned and pushed the door closed. He could hear the sound of her rapid breathing, sense the fear in her quick movements.

"You've got to help me!" she gasped as she turned back to face him, her shoulders pressed against the door. In the gloom she was only a pale, ghostly figure. "You've got to get me away from here!"

Ronnie found his voice. "I'll do my best, ma'am," he said automatically. "But I'm not sure I'm in any sort of position to be of much help."

His easygoing manner seemed to reassure her. He realized she was almost as apprehensive of him as she was of whatever had driven her here. She'd had no idea what sort of man he was when she'd come blindly seeking his aid.

"Who are you, ma'am?" he asked.

"My name's Mindy Simmons," she answered, then shushed him for a second time. For long moments they listened, but there was no outcry from the camp.

"No one saw me," she concluded aloud with evident relief. She still hadn't quite caught her breath. "Just a minute; I'm going to strike a match."

She fumbled, then a spark flared into a tiny flame that made Ronnie blink. She hunched over the match, shielding its glow from the window in the wall behind her. Ronnie let his breath out hard enough to make the flame waver as he got his first look at her face.

She was lovely in the wan light. Her delicate features were framed by pale blond hair that fell to her shoulders and sparkled with glints of gold from the flame. But exhaustion and despair had dimmed the loveliness. A dark bruise marred one smooth cheek.

"Are you all right?" she asked, and he saw that she had been gazing at his battered features, had even extended a hand partway toward his face. "I know they beat you."

"I'm fine," Ronnie said hoarsely. "Better get that match out."

She pursed her lips and extinguished it with a soft exhalation of her breath. In the sudden darkness the image of her bruised loveliness still seemed to hover before Ronnie's vision.

"How did you get here?" he asked blankly.

She moved closer to him, as though seeking comfort or reassurance, and he wondered how it would've felt if she had actually touched his face a moment earlier.

"Some rustlers stole our cattle down in Indian Territory." Her voice voice fell even softer. "When we tried to stop them, they killed my parents, then took me with them. They brought me here, and Sedge Tallant made them give me to him. He won't let me leave. I have to do the cooking, and other things." Ronnie sensed rather than saw her shudder.

It was easy enough to fill in the gaps in what she said. Ronnie felt his mouth tighten. This gal had had a rough go of it. He felt a sudden harebrained impulse to take her in his arms and draw her protectively to his chest. "I'll get you out of here," he vowed instead, even though he still didn't have any idea how he could manage it.

"I knew you were different from Tallant and the rest when I saw them bring you in," she spoke with evident relief. "I was certain of it when I saw your face. I could tell you're a decent man. I had to come here. I can't stand being in this place any longer. It's so awful. I thought maybe you could help me, and together we could escape! Here, I brought you this.''

From somewhere she produced a small bundle and pressed it toward him. He felt the warm brush of her hands as his fingers closed on the familiar leather and metal of a gun belt, the holster sagging heavy with a pistol.

''I got this from Tallant's quarters,'' she whispered by way of explanation. ''It's an extra one. He told me he killed the man who wore it.'' Her voice quavered.

Eagerly Ronnie took the belt. He withdrew the pistol, examining it by feel. A .45, he figured. Opening the loading gate, he turned the cylinder, running his thumb over the cartridges. All six chambers were loaded. He wouldn't know if it would actually fire unless he was forced to use it.

He snugged the belt tight about his waist and adjusted the holster so that it hung halfway between wrist and elbow. The gun slid easily in and out of its holster. It had seen a lot of use. He wondered who the former owner—Tallant's victim—had been. He realized she was watching his silhouette in the darkness.

''You're with him, aren't you?'' came her voice. ''I mean Stark, the one they call the Peacemaker.''

''Yeah, I'm with him,'' Ronnie told her, then amended dryly, ''Or, I was.''

''They're all scared of him. Even Tallant, though he won't admit it.''

''I am too, a little bit,'' Ronnie confessed. ''But I sure wouldn't mind seeing him about now.''

"Are you like him?" she queried hesitantly. "A gunfighter?"

Ronnie gave a muffled snort of laughter. "Naw, I'm just a two-bit mustanger."

Unexpectedly he felt the quick pressure of her hand on his arm. Then it was gone. "I'm glad you're not a gunfighter."

Her words thrilled him. But he didn't let himself consider what all they might mean. "Before we're done, you could be wishing I was a lot more like Stark," he said gruffly.

He saw her shake her head. Her pale hair seemed to shimmer in the darkness. He resisted another loco urge to reach out and touch its silky softness, then booted himself mentally for acting like some moon-struck yokel. If they were going to have any chance of getting out of here, he was going to have to get his mind off his fetching and vulnerable companion.

And they didn't have much of a chance, he acknowledged grimly to himself. "Where's Tallant?" he asked aloud.

"He's asleep."

"Are there any guards nearby?"

"No. There's one in the watchtower, and two or three of them are on patrol just inside the fence."

Ronnie mulled it over.

"We can get horses from the stable," Mindy pressed on. "We must hurry!"

Ronnie sensed in her voice a little of the desperation it must've taken to drive her here to seek help from a complete stranger who was himself a prisoner. He also understood just how much she was relying on him.

"We'll get moving in a minute," he assured her with more confidence than he felt. "Guess you ought to know, my name's Ronnie Hall."

His matter-of-factness appeared to calm her nerves once more. He asked a few other questions, then fell silent again, chewing worriedly at his lower lip.

"Your friend—Mr. Stark," she ventured. "Can he help us?"

"I don't reckon Jim Stark would run out on a compadre," Ronnie answered. "But there doesn't seem to be much he could do to get us out of here." Which meant, he added silently, that it was up to him.

With the thought came resolve. He crossed to the door and, gun in hand, inched it open. He was conscious of her close behind him, and even fancied he caught some faint flowery scent off her.

He had a view of a slice of the shadowy interior of the compound. There were no torches or lanterns. He figured Tallant had elected to keep the camp in darkness so as not give Stark any targets for his big rifle. So, maybe Stark was helping them after all.

He jerked his head for her to follow, and slipped out of the prison shed. The night air felt cool after the stuffiness of the cell. He stayed in the shadows, waiting and listening, trying to locate the guards. He could hear Mindy breathing at his back.

At last he spotted one of the hardcases strolling along the base of the opposite wall, rifle cradled in his arms. As the first guard's shadowy form moved on, Ronnie saw another figure materialize, headed toward the first. They met and looked to be shooting the breeze for a moment. Then they parted to continue on their rounds.

That accounted for two, at any rate. Ronnie didn't know if there were any more, but he and his charge couldn't afford to stand around here all night. The stable was set in the center of the fortress, which meant they could keep to the shadows until they got near it. Then, however, they'd have to cross several yards of open ground.

Without thinking about it, Ronnie reached a hand backward. Immediately he felt the intimate grasp of Mindy's fingers. With her hand entwined in his, he led her stealthily among the shadows of the smaller outbuildings. He halted to keep a storage shed between them and one of the patrolling sentries. Their breathing, his own heartbeat, and the creak of his sore muscles when he shifted his weight all seemed unnaturally loud to him. His gun hand was sweating so badly he wondered if he'd even be able to fire the weapon should the need arise.

The guard passed by. Ronnie felt Mindy squeeze his hand. He squeezed back, whether to reassure her or himself he didn't know. Maybe both.

Once more he led out. They reached the point opposite the door to the stable. The gate stood open. That was a bit of luck. He couldn't see into the blackness of the central corridor, but he knew it was lined on either side with stalls, some of which held horses. Other horses were penned outside the far end. There was no way they could get to those horses without stirring up a ruckus. They would have to rely on whatever animals and gear they found inside.

A horse snorted and pawed at the door of its stall. Another answered. The sounds carried clearly but didn't seem to arouse the interest of the sentries. Another piece of luck. They could get away with a little bit of noise once they were in the stable. Ronnie offered a silent prayer of thanks, then added a supplication for the additional and even greater luck they'd need to get inside the stable at all.

He glanced at the looming shape of the watchtower. He couldn't make out the sentry in the darkness atop it. He hoped the yahoo was paying more attention to the surrounding countryside than he was to the interior of the compound.

There was no time like the present. "Come on!" he hissed, and ran with her out across the open space toward the stable. He half expected to hear the blast of a rifle and feel the impact of a slug, but they plunged unharmed into the darkness, and drew up panting.

No outcry sounded. There was only the noise of their breathing and the snort and stomp of the horses in the stalls. Their hands were still clasped.

"We made it!" Mindy cried in a loud whisper, and abruptly she was hugging him impulsively. His own arms tightened automatically about her slim form. He felt her softness, the surprising strength of her arms, and the brush of her silky hair against his stubbled cheek.

Embarrassed suddenly, fearing he had somehow taken advantage of her, he released her. She stepped back, and he opened his mouth for some kind of apology.

"What the deuce?" a coarse male voice growled from the blackness farther inside the stable.

Mindy gasped as Ronnie whirled. He could barely make out the shape of a man emerging from the open door of a stall. Maybe the fellow had been sleeping there; Ronnie didn't know. It sure didn't matter much now.

"You're the kid they hauled in this morning!"

Recognition was all the hardcase needed. Ronnie saw the arm of his dark form move. His own hand came up to the butt of the Colt in the holster Mindy had given him. He had time for only a fractional second's awareness that if he messed up now, it would be all over for him, and Mindy would be condemned once more to a life of degradation. Other than that, he didn't think at all. He pulled the Colt as his arm came up. It wasn't fast, but it was smooth and sure.

Groggy from sleep, the hardcase fumbled his draw. He cursed, and Ronnie, still smooth and sure, drove a bullet square into his shadowy figure. The gunman's pistol stabbed a roaring flame into the dirt of the stable floor. The gun flashes were blinding, and the thunder of the shots boomed against the walls of the stable. The imprisoned horses went wild.

The hardcase crumpled. Ronnie wheeled toward the doorway, pushing Mindy behind him with a sweep of his arm.

Now, he knew, there'd be the devil himself to pay.

Chapter Eleven

James Stark frowned and thumb-snapped the wooden match into life. The tiny flame flared in the night's darkness. It would make him a target for some sharpshooter in the compound if he planned to hold it for very long.

He didn't.

Grimly he flicked it into the buffalo grass. It arced down like a tiny meteor. Still dry from the end of the summer heat, the grass caught quickly. The slight breeze at Stark's back pushed the flames on their way.

Satisfied, Stark kneed Red on a dozen feet and sent another match spinning to the ground. It too caught. At a fast canter, then, he covered a good quarter of a mile, flicking matches as he went. When he reined up and looked back, an uneven line of flame was picking up speed as it swept across the grassland. In its path was the black shape of the outlaw fortress.

Stark despised using fire as a weapon. It afflicted the innocent and the guilty alike. In these vast grasslands, a fire could race for miles, devouring pasture, stock, homesteads, and even whole communities, if left unchecked. But with Ronnie a prisoner, any assault he made on Tallant's compound had to be single-handed. And it had to be fast, before Tallant finished

113

with the mustanger and dug him a grave alongside those of the gunmen who had fallen to Stark's rifle. Fire was the only weapon Stark had that could serve his purpose.

And there was still no guarantee of success. In fact, the odds were all against it. But he had to try, and he could only hope that the dampness from the recent thunderstorm he'd seen pass over the area beyond the compound would keep the fire from spreading too far.

The blaze was moving fast. The tang of smoke stung his nostrils. He put Red into a reckless gallop to get behind the encampment before the fire reached its wooden palisades. He knew he didn't have long before the advancing blaze was spotted and an alarm raised.

He had even less time than he'd expected, he realized as two muffled shots, one on top of the other, sounded from within the fortress. A falling-out among thieves? Ronnie's death knell? He didn't know, but the camp would be coming to life now, and the fire was sure to be spotted. He put heels hard to Red's ribs.

He heard a startled shout from nearby, and saw two mounted shapes take form out of the gloom. He'd crossed the path of a pair of outriders. Guns blazing, they bore down on him.

Stark hauled Red up hard and whipped the shotgun from its sheath. He jacked the lever and brought the butt to his shoulder. Bullets were flying wild around him, and one of them slashed along Red's flank. Not even rigid training could make a horse stand still for that. Startled, hurt, the big sorrel shied wildly.

Stark was almost flung from the saddle. He clamped his thighs tight around the barrel of the horse's body, and for a frantic moment he was juggling the reins and the shotgun, the latter in his left hand. There was no way to fire the shotgun one-handed. He jammed the sweat-tasting reins between his teeth and bit down hard, freeing his right hand so he could wipe the .45 from leather.

He jerked back hard with his head to tighten the reins. Red's surging lessened beneath him. Then the charging outlaws were upon him, trying to ride him down or blast him out of the saddle. They tangled in a mass of bucking, biting horses and yelling, shooting men.

A pistol seemed to explode in Stark's face. Left-handed, he swung the shotgun savagely at a dimly seen shape. The shock of impact all but tore the weapon out of his grip. The shape fell away beneath the trampling hooves and cried out sharply. Red lunged against the remaining owlhoot's horse. Stark thrust the Colt forward and felt its barrel sink into flesh. He pulled the trigger. The panic-stricken mount raced away as its rider tumbled backward out of the saddle.

Red jerked to a trembling halt. Stark was trembling some himself. He didn't know how he'd survived that gun blast at point-blank range. His eyes and face felt as though they'd been seared by a branding iron.

Both outriders lay still. Stark took time only for a reassuring pat to Red's sweat-dampened neck before he put the sorrel into motion again. Tending the bullet crease would have to wait. The fracas had lasted only seconds, but they were seconds he could ill afford to spare.

Commotion was rising within the compound. More gunshots erupted there. Somebody yelled about the on-rushing fire. Stark was grateful for whatever gun trouble had added to the ruckus. He brought Red to a skidding halt close beside the fence on the far side of the fortress, away from the fire. He slid the shotgun's sling over his shoulder, caught the tops of two of the sharpened poles, and vaulted lithely out of the saddle, clearing the fence with ease. His legs bent to take the impact of his landing. He sank the rest of the way to one knee, ducking his head as he slipped the shotgun off his shoulder. Automatically he levered a shell into place.

The blaze had already reached the far wall. The dry wood made ready tender. Flames crackled and leaped higher than the wall in several places. Smoke was beginning to drift through the camp in a dark gray haze. Somebody was trying with little success to organize a bucket brigade from the water trough under the windmill. Cattle were bellowing outside the compound. The pens wouldn't last long under the weight of the spooked beeves. Sporadic gunfire flared and cracked near the stable.

Stark didn't know where Ronnie might be. He'd spent most of the daylight hours lying low and evading the organized hunt Tallant had mounted for him. He'd had no chance to observe what went on in the fortress. The pitched gunfight near the stable drew him now.

In a crouch, shotgun held ready at waist level, he worked his way in that direction. The flames were clawing at the palisade, casting a diffused light through the haze of smoke and dust. Sparks danced in the air stirred by the flames. It was only a matter of time till fire took hold on some of the wooden structures within the walls.

Tallant. Where was Tallant? Stark wondered. The gun boss was the most dangerous of his enemies. But he was nowhere to be seen.

A man ran past, his strides awkward in his horseman's boots. Stark's hands tightened on the shotgun, but the hombre had other business on his mind than worrying about intruders in the compound. He paid no heed to Stark's presence. Stark let him go. There was no need for more killing—yet.

Emboldened, he pressed on. Skittish horses roamed at will. Ahead he saw that the fire had gained a grip on the high roof of the stable. Flames leaped and crackled and crawled rapidly across the unpainted wood. A number of men poured gunfire from various points of cover into the dark interior of the building. An occasional gunflame stabbed back at them. Whoever was in there had forted himself up right good, but with the flames eating at the roof, the end of the gun battle was coming soon.

For a handful of moments Stark paused in the shadows just outside of the illumination of the leaping flames. Smoke stung his eyes. Blinking, he made a mental tally of the gunsels assaulting the stable. His throat felt raw.

It had to be Ronnie pinned down in there. Somehow the scrappy wrangler had almost managed to win his way free. But now, caught between fire and bullets, he was fast running out of time and luck.

Stark stepped out of the darkness and fired from the hip. The solid load tore the nearest gunman from where he crouched and flung him sprawling into the dust. Beyond him, another hardcase whirled in surprise, swinging his six-gun automatically to bear. Stark worked the lever and pulled the trigger again. The gunslinger went down in a spreading spray of buckshot.

Wreathed in smoke, Stark stalked through the flame-lit darkness. The shotgun bucked and roared in his fists and belched its own deadly fire. Men reeled and died. Some managed to shoot back, but the panicked shots ripped harmlessly past Stark as he dealt death among them. He knelt to reload, then strode on, firing with cold, ruthless efficiency.

The last two men broke and ran, scrambling away to be lost in the dark and smoke. Stark stopped. The shotgun was hot in his grip. His head swiveled back and forth. No one else was paying any attention to him. The outlaws and gunmen left were busy vainly fighting the fire or trying to catch the loose horses in the compound. Likely whoever was hemmed in the stable had turned the animals out to provide a distraction, or to save them from the flames.

As Stark watched he saw one yahoo tangle his fingers in the mane of an animal, scramble astride it, and, bareback, hightail it for the prairie. That hombre had had enough.

Stark looked toward the stable just in time to see a reeling figure stagger out of the smoke. Sure enough, he recognized Ronnie. The wrangler paused and bent forward, hands dropping to his knees. He gasped for breath. Then he straightened, drew one more convulsive draught of fresh air, and, turning, plunged back into the maw of the burning stable. Stark's shout of protest went unheeded.

Stark laid the shotgun aside and ran forward. He hadn't set the plains on fire and killed this many men just to let the mustanger go to his death like some loco maverick.

Heat washed over him as he neared the wide doorway. Inside he could see the flicker of flames through the smoke. It was a wonder Ronnie had stood it as long as he had. What on earth had possessed him to go back in that inferno?

Stark tugged his kerchief up over his mouth and nose, ducked his head, and darted forward. The smoke and heat swallowed him. He groped through searing, choking darkness, stumbled over something, and caught himself on outflung hands. Close to the floor the air was a little better. He managed to shout Ronnie's name aloud.

The hellish glare of flames was overhead and to either side of him. In fancy's eye he pictured the flaming roof collapsing atop him. He crawled forward, shouted again, and thought he heard a muffled response over the hacking cough his voice had given way to.

He lurched upright, crouching, and blundered against the front of a stall. He felt the harsh heat of the wood burn through his shirt, and recoiled away. A croaking noise sounded almost at his feet. He reached down. His fumbling fingers encountered a kneeling human form pawing weakly at something on the floor.

"Help—" Ronnie's voice was a tortured rasp.

Stark groped further. He understood with sudden shock that the wrangler was struggling to move the inert form of a woman sprawled in the dirt.

Stark didn't question how this had come about. He heaved the woman erect, supporting her with Ronnie's faltering help. Together, gasping and staggering, they hauled her toward the doorway. Stark clawed through the smoke, and they lunged at last out into the cooler night air.

As they hobbled farther from the stable its flaming roof gave way at last. The whole building folded like a house of cards touched by a lighted match. A wave of heat tore at them. Flame and smoke and cinders flared high and then subsided.

Stark blinked at the ragged scarecrow figure of the wrangler. The younger man made a frantic gesture at their human burden. Stark saw it was the young blond girl he had seen held apparent prisoner in the outlaw camp. She was still breathing, he detected as he knelt awkwardly beside her. Something had knocked her senseless. Her pretty face was smudged with soot.

"She'll make it," Stark said.

"Thank God!" Ronnie managed reverently. He shook his head, coughed, and stammered on. "We couldn't get out the rear because of the fire. I let the horses loose; wanted to try riding two of them out. One knocked her down. I couldn't leave her there."

Stark straightened tiredly to his feet. Then the smoke-thickened voice of Sedge Tallant bawled from behind him. "Peacemaker! Blast you! I knew this was your doing. By the devil, I'll take you down for it! Draw!"

Stark's entire body pivoted to his right in a single motion, all exhausation sloughing from him under the savage lash of danger. His gun hand, tight at his side, came around first, the .45 blasting once and twice even before he'd completed the turn. He fired one more time as he came fully about. With the first two he'd been aiming by the sound of Tallant's voice. With the third he finally got a look at his opponent.

Tallant had been staggered backward. He stayed on his feet long enough to give Stark one disbelieving shake of his head, then he folded to the ground.

"Land sakes! What kind of a draw was that?" Ronnie blurted.

Stark spat to clear his throat. "One I didn't teach you."

He stiffened his legs so they wouldn't tremble, and paced forward to stand over the fallen gun boss. Tallant had given him a chance. Why, he didn't know. Could be it had been professional pride that kept him from shooting the Peacemaker in the back. Whatever the reason, it had meant his undoing. Two bullets— Stark thought the last two—had caught him. Tallant had bossed his last gun crew.

Stark looked about. The whole compound was a conflagration, with reddish orange flames leaping triumphantly up into the night. What hardcases hadn't died had fled.

Stark holstered his Colt and turned his gaze back toward Ronnie. "This about what you all hired me to do?" he drawled.

Chapter Twelve

"I've been told," Prudence McKay stated accusingly, "that you've been interfering in the affairs of Randall Burke."

Stark stared at her where she stood formal and unyielding in front of his desk. He had risen to his feet when she came unannounced into his office.

"You've been told," he repeated carefully. "Just who was it who told you?"

"Randall Burke himself," she answered crisply. "Is it true?"

Stark gestured at a chair. "Sit down; you're making me tired."

"I'll stand, thank you." Her tone was icy.

"Suit yourself." Stark dropped into his swivel chair and regarded her for a beat longer.

She met his gaze with a glare. "You've been gone almost a month." She made it another accusation.

"On business," Stark explained levelly.

"Did that business involve Randall Burke?"

"Why did Burke come to you?" Stark parried.

For the first time he thought he detected a trace of defensiveness. "Why shouldn't he? After all, he's my client. I am his lawyer."

Stark pressed what little advantage he had. "Just what did he tell you about his affairs?"

"That he runs a cattle brokerage business in the Unassigned Lands," Prudence advised tightly. "Now, answer me. Did you interfere in his operation there?"

"Burned it to the ground," Stark confessed placidly.

Outrage flared in Prudence's eyes. She drew herself up even straighter. "What right do you have—?" she burst out.

"They were stolen cattle, Pru," Stark interrupted gently. It was the first time he had ever used the shorter more intimate form of her name. "Burke sells stolen cattle that he buys from rustlers who prey on the small ranches in the Indian Lands. Burke's worse than the rustlers. Without him, they couldn't operate as effectively as they do. Or did," he added.

Stricken, Prudence stared at him. "Are you certain of this?" she snapped.

Piqued suddenly, Stark leaned back in his chair. "I've got a couple of witnesses who'll be along in a few minutes, if my word's not good enough for you," he said growling. "One of the men who hired me, and a young woman who was held prisoner by Burke's gun boss. She can probably provide a detailed listing of various other sordid crimes you can lay at your client's feet."

Prudence looked quickly away. Still not meeting his gaze, she stepped back and sank into one of the chairs in front of his desk. She looked very small in it.

"Several of the ranchers hired me to stop what was happening," Stark went on more equably. "They had no one else to turn to. There's no law up there. The only way to stop it was with the methods I used."

At last Prudence turned her face toward him. Her eyes were bright. ''I'm terribly sorry, Jim,'' she said with obvious sincerity. ''I should've known you wouldn't break the law or interfere in the business matters of an honest man.'' She actually lifted one hand and bit at a fingernail before she caught herself and jerked her hand back to her lap.

Her contrition nudged Stark with an odd unease. He explained the circumstances further, omitting much of the detail of his campaign against Tallant and his crew. Prudence listened raptly.

The prairie fire had burned itself out with little damage to anything beyond the compound. Mindy had recovered consciousness, although she was weak from her ordeal. At Ronnie's invite, both she and Stark had stayed at his ranch to rest for a few days. Stark had given Ronnie and his neighbors a hand in rounding up the rustled cattle and returning them to their owners.

Once that task was completed, Stark suggested that Mindy return to Guthrie with him to get some proper medical care and take steps to settle her parents' estate. She had looked questioningly at Ronnie for guidance before agreeing. Stark wasn't surprised to have Ronnie volunteer to accompany them. The wrangler could barely seem to take his eyes off the young woman, or do enough to see to her welfare.

They had reached the territorial capital the preceding day. Stark had put the couple up in separate rooms at his hotel. He had barely gotten settled in his office that morning when Prudence made her unexpected appearance.

She shook her head in wonder when he finished.

"That poor girl," she said, then looked anxiously at Stark. "Were you hurt?"

Stark smiled. "I'm fine. Ronnie took a little roughing up, but he's gotten over it. Both of them ought to be showing up here shortly. I wanted to get Mindy in touch with you so you could help her settle her folks' affairs."

"Of course I'll help her," Prudence promised. Then her pretty lips drew down. "The nerve of Randall Burke," she said tightly.

"I'm still not sure why he came whining to you in the first place," Stark commented. "Or why you believed him."

A flustered look crossed her face. "He wasn't sure of your motives," she offered vaguely. "He thought there might be some sort of legal action to be taken against you." As she spoke she turned a comely pink from her neck to the roots of her hair.

Stark stared at her, musing over her first response. "Burke thought I was doing it just to get back at him," he said with dawning comprehension. "And you thought it might be personal too! Did you really believe I had it in for that overstuffed tinhorn because of that night at the Golden Apple?"

Prudence's chin came up defiantly. "Was any of it for personal reasons?" she demanded.

Stark tilted his head back and grinned with huge enjoyment. "Well," he admitted lazily, "I have to confess I took a certain amount of personal satisfaction out of dismantling his sorry operation, and getting paid for the privilege of doing it."

Prudence's cheeks flamed fiery red. "I was right!"

she exclaimed. "It was personal! James Stark, how dare you? Even if he deserved it, you had no right to start a private vendetta over—"

The opening of the outer office door, and Ronnie Hall's cheery hello shushed her as effectively as a hand clapped over her mouth, but the glower she threw at Stark told him in no uncertain terms that he hadn't heard the last of her views on private vendettas.

But Prudence was charming and graceful as she greeted Ronnie and was introduced to Mindy. The mustanger's bruises were fading, and he acted as chipper as ever. There was a fond gleam in his eye whenever his glance fell on his companion.

As for Mindy, much of the despairing and broken spirit that Stark had seen in her back at the outlaw fortress had faded, although a trace of it still remained far back in her eyes. She'd be a long time losing that, Stark reckoned.

But in the days since her liberation she had blossomed physically and spiritually. Her comely face was radiant, and she made a fetching sight in a new blue dress, with a bonnet perched on the bun of her silky blond hair.

Prudence ushered her into the outer office while Ronnie confirmed that the final installment of Stark's fee was being wired to his bank. Shortly Prudence reappeared to advise that Mindy was to accompany her to her office to discuss her parents' estate. It only took a brief moment of eye contact between Mindy and Ronnie for him to say he'd go along eagerly. Stark saw them out of his office, studiously ignoring the final look Prudence gave him in passing.

He returned to his desk and started sorting through the stack of paperwork Mae, his office manager, had left for his attention. He heard the outer office door open and figured Mae had arrived for work. Automatically he glanced toward the small mirror positioned so as to give him a view of the lobby area.

It wasn't Mae. Tension tightened the muscles of Stark's back, but what was almost a grin pulled at his mouth. He slid the drawer on his right open to reveal a short-barreled version of the Colt .45 Peacemaker within easy reach. His regular Colt was holstered at his side, but drawing while sitting down was always a tricky proposition. He had his face impassive by the time his visitors appeared in the doorway to his office.

Big and arrogant, dressed in a fancy suit, Randall Burke strode into the room. Once again, there was no sign of a gun, Stark noted. Chin, the renegade Chinese bodyguard, drifted on cat's feet in his wake, silent even in his heavy clodhopper shoes. His dark eyes sought those of Stark over the shoulder of his boss. He settled his shoulders against the wall by the door and leaned there, arms crossed. Stark wondered what was concealed under the cheap oversize suit coat he wore.

Burke halted in front of Stark's desk. A cigar jutted from between his teeth. Smoke trailed upward from its tip. ''Welcome back to Guthrie,'' he spoke around the cigar. His tone was as sour as the smoke from his stogie.

''Always good to be home among friends,'' Stark said dryly.

The cigar jerked up and down. "I suppose your employers are happy."

"My employers are always happy," Stark claimed blandly.

Burke's gaze traveled past Stark to the guns displayed on the wall. "I know you used that shotgun you favor," he began, "But what'd you use for the long-range shooting? That big Winchester there?" He stabbed the cigar at the Sporting Rifle now resting once more in its place of honor.

Stark didn't take his eyes off the other man. "I only use that for big game."

"Human game?"

Casually Stark slid his hand along the desktop until it rested directly above the .45 nestled in the drawer. "Just what are you talking about?"

Burke thrust his big shoulders forward. The cigar bobbed fiercely in his teeth. "I'm talking about a dead gun boss, a compound burned to the ground, and a lot of good men killed or run out of the country!"

"Bad breaks," Stark offered. "The Good Book says that the rain falls on the just and the unjust. Reckon you fit in there somewhere."

So Burke had gotten a thorough report of what had happened, he reflected to himself. He'd even had time to inspect the damage personally.

Abruptly Burke pivoted away from the desk. He stood for a moment, his back half to Stark, staring out the window. The cigar jerked up and down, and balls of smoke puffed angrily up from it. Chin shifted his shoulders slightly where he leaned near the door. One foot was now flat against the wall, and one of his hands was out of sight.

"All right, Stark." Burke wheeled back to face him. "You did your job. I can probably even take a good guess at who hired you to do it. You're in this for the money. I can understand that. I'm a businessman too. I don't like you, and you don't cotton to me, but we don't have to like each other to do business. Savvy?"

Stark frowned and cocked his head to one side.

Burke took it for assent. He grunted with satisfaction. "We can talk turkey. You shut my operation down, but that doesn't mean you necessarily put me out of business for good in no-man's-land. I had a sweet deal going there."

"Not anymore," Stark reminded.

"Not now, anyway," Burke concurred. "But tomorrow could tell a different story. And if it does, and if those no-account ranchers come back and want you sticking your six-shooter into my affairs, why, you just let me know."

"What happens then?"

Burke's grin was hard and tight as the teeth of a sprung bear trap. "You worked for them once; next time you can work for me. Whatever they offer you, I'll up the ante. All you have to do to earn your pay is sit right here in your office, or go work another job; makes no difference to me." Burke paused and shifted the cigar from one side of his mouth to the other. "Well, what do you say?"

Stark leaned forward across his desk. "There are some things I won't do for money," he said deliberately, "Like shoot an innocent man in the back, burn down an orphanage, or work for you. Do *you* savvy?"

Burke's handsome face turned ugly. Stark saw no signal or gesture, but Chin came smoothly away from the wall, propelled by the foot he'd pressed there. He pivoted to take two quick steps forward, then halted, feet shoulder width apart, arms still crossed.

Stark spoke crisply. "Turn your pet hatchetman loose in here and I'll drill him before he moves. And I'll get you next."

Burke made a single sharp gesture toward Chin. The Chinaman showed no emotion. As ever, his face was as blank as a fence post. But he retreated two precise steps and stood unmoving.

"It might be fun to watch you try your gun against Chin. You know your luck hasn't been too good against him in the past. And your luck might not be too good against me either."

"Well, now, your luck hasn't been too good up in no-man's-land, has it?"

"You weren't playing against me in no-man's-land," Burke said flatly. "You were going up against Tallant, and he was nothing but a fancy gun slick just like you. From now on it's a different game, with different rules, and different odds. Believe me, you won't like any of it."

"You're wrong, Burke. This isn't a game anymore. Maybe it never was. There's no rules, and there's no odds; there's just living or dying. That's the only kind of business I'll do with you."

"You called it. That's the way we'll play." Burke wheeled and strode toward the door. Chin sidestepped from his path, then fell in behind him. In the mirror, Stark saw them leave.

After a moment he slid the gun drawer closed. He recalled Stu Hollingshed's bitter prediction that shutting down Burke's operation was only a temporary solution, and that Burke would just start it up again. It looked like the cattleman had been right.

And just now, Stark knew, he himself had been wrong. He had his own rules, but if he abided by them, Burke would win. The only way to stop Burke now, if he was going to stop him at all, was to step outside the law.

Chapter Thirteen

"Good morning, Mr. Stark."

Stark drew up in surprise in the hallway outside his office. "Morning, Mindy," he said. "And you know by now, it's Jim, not Mr. Stark."

She flushed prettily and ducked her head in acknowledgment. Stark sensed her embarrassment at having him find her here waiting for him first thing in the morning. He held his peace as he unlocked the door and saw her into his inner office.

"Have a seat, Mindy. What can I do for you?"

Outwardly the past six weeks in Guthrie seemed to have allowed her to make a complete recovery from her ordeal at the hands of the outlaws. Even the haunted cast of her eyes had all but disappeared. He'd seen little of her lately, which made her appearance here at his doorstep all the more puzzling.

Once she was seated, she still looked to be nervous and uncomfortable. Stark hesitated, then took one of the other straight back chairs in front of the desk so things wouldn't be quite so formal. This appeared to fluster her even more. She shifted about on the hard seat of the chair.

"Job going all right?" he asked awkwardly.

She flashed a quick smile, as though relieved to

have a topic to talk about. ''Oh, yes. I've always been good at sewing, and Prudence was so wonderful to get me a job at that dress shop.''

Stark hadn't seen much of Prudence lately either, not since their scene in his office upon his return from no-man's-land. He'd been out of town for a spell, and had returned earlier in the week to find a letter from her awaiting him. It tersely advised him of the tentative date of the trial at which he was to be her expert witness, and went on to state that she would be in touch with him prior to that time to review his testimony. So far, she hadn't made contact.

And here was Mindy sitting forlornly in his office while he tried to figure out what in tarnation she wanted. Where was Prudence when he needed her?

''Can I get you some coffee?'' he tried another tack.

''No, thank you. I don't care for any.'' She stiffened her spine then and met his gaze. ''Have you heard that Ronnie's supposed to be arriving back in town today?''

''Yeah. I got a wire saying he and Hollingshed and Bishop needed to meet with me.'' Stark had an unpleasant notion what that meeting might be about, but for the moment he was more puzzled over his visitor's attitude. ''You don't seem real excited about getting to see him again,'' he ventured aloud.

''Oh, but I am!'' she contradicted fervently. ''We've written each other back and forth since he returned to his ranch, and his letters are so sweet. I've really been looking forward to him coming back here. I'm sure I'll be so nervous that I'll make a terrible fool of myself when I see him again. I think—'' She broke off to blush a cheery red, then went on with evident joy, ''I think he's going to ask me to marry him!''

''Congratulations!'' Stark grinned. ''It's about time he got around to putting his loop on you. Just let me know if he doesn't pop the question, and I'll prod him along so he stops wasting time and gets down to business.''

To his surprise, her joy faded away into painful concern. ''That's . . . that's what I wanted to talk to you about, Mr. Stark; I mean, Jim.''

''About getting hitched?'' Stark said, more puzzled than ever.

She nodded a quick yes. ''That's right.''

For some reason the image of Prudence McKay's pretty face flashed across Stark's mind. ''I'm no authority on marriage,'' he protested.

''But you're a man.'' She plunged boldly on now that she was committed to her course. ''That's why I need to talk to you.''

Stark was starting to wish for a trigger-happy gunman to deal with rather than this perplexing female. He couldn't think of anything much to say, so he only nodded weakly.

Mindy wet her lips. ''It's about what happened to me in no-man's-land.'' Her voice was timorous. ''I'm sure Ronnie loves me, and I know I love him.'' Her embarrassment deepened. ''But I keep thinking that I'm not good enough for him, that he'll think less of me, or not really want me. Prudence has told me that if we love each other, and work at our marriage, then none of it will matter in the long run, and I want so hard to believe her. But she's a woman, and I just had to talk to someone else, to a man I could trust. So I came to you." She bowed her head. There was the gleam of tears on her smooth cheek.

Stark wondered how he'd ever gotten cast in the role of giving advice to the lovelorn. But at least this was an easy enough problem as far as he was concerned.

"Listen to me, Mindy." He used his thumb and forefinger to tilt her chin up until she faced him. She sniffled, but didn't look away. "Ronnie's a good, God-fearing man. You know that." He was rewarded with a timid nod. "Well, no decent man is going to think any the less of you because of what happened. Ronnie's not going to hold it against you; you shouldn't go on holding it against yourself."

Her eyes widened with obvious hope. "You're sure?" she stammered.

"I'm sure. And if Ronnie's fool enough to let you slip out of his loop, then there'll be a whole passel of other decent fellows waiting in line to be your beau. Why, I might even show up on your front porch myself."

He grinned to let her know he was just joshing, and it worked, because she broke into a wide smile of her own. Fumbling in her handbag, she produced a frilly handkerchief and wiped the tears from her eyes. In moments she was all youthful high spirits.

"Oh," she exclaimed as he saw her thankfully to thc door, "I almost forgot. Ronnie said in his last letter for me to meet him here at noon to go to lunch. He figured you all would be through talking business by then."

With her gone, Stark brooded briefly over his up-coming meeting with his clients. He hadn't crossed paths with Randall Burke lately, and he had started to hope the restaurant owner had decided to cut his losses in the Unassigned Lands and leave matters there well enough alone. But the ranchers' visit didn't bode well for that being the case.

And, sure enough, it wasn't the case, he found out for certain later that morning.

"I told all of you what would happen," Stu Hollingshed announced with bitter satisfaction. "Yeah, Stark here shut down Burke's operation for a spell, but, like I said, there's nothing to keep him from getting it up and running again." He turned to his comrades seated beside him. "Well, did I hit the nail on the head, or didn't I?"

"Just tell me what Burke's done," Stark cut in.

Cass Bishop's broad face showed his relief at not having to resume what was plainly an ongoing topic of talk among them. Ronnie, his bruises completely gone had the air of a man with more important business on his mind. He jumped eagerly to fill in the gaps for Stark.

"We done got word that there's a pack of hardcases gathering in no-man's-land. For a while there, after you wiped out that camp, the rustling plumb near petered out. Now, though, looks like it's starting up again.

"I rode up to have a look-see myself, and stumbled on a brace of gun slicks drifting down from Kansas. Ornery-looking cusses. I played it dumb, like I might be open to some shady work myself. They mostly treated me as if I was some kind of tenderfoot." He scowled at the memory. "But one of them let slip they'd heard somebody was doing some big-time hiring in those parts. That was good enough for me, and I rode out. When I got back to my homeplace, Cass here told me he'd already lost a few beeves to wide loopers."

Bishop nodded soberly. "For a fact."

"I'll go back and clear out the varmints before they get dug in," Stark said. "Eventually Burke'll get tired of losing men and money, and he'll pull in his horns." Privately Stark wondered if he was right.

Hollingshed plainly had doubts as well. "So we pay you all over again, and keep paying you the next time and the next. By Godfrey, eventually you'll cost us more than the consarned rustlers."

"On the house," Stark bluntly, forestalling an angry outburst from Ronnie directed at Hollingshed. "You can keep your money."

This time there was no pleasure or satisfaction in taking the job. He wasn't wanting to dedicate the rest of his life, or keep risking it for that matter, to put Randall Burke out of business.

He sat back in his desk chair and listened to the three of them rehash things once more. Ronnie was all for taking out after the latest batch of recruited gunslingers before they got organized. Cass Bishop was willing to concede reluctantly that such a course was necessary. Hollingshed only wanted to gloat and demand impossible assurances of success.

The murmur of feminine voices came from the outer office. Mae must be greeting Mindy, Stark supposed.

He didn't bother to look at the mirror. It must be near noon. That suited him fine. He was ready for this confab to end.

But Hollingshed seemed intent on going back over the entire problem. "Sure, we can send our hired gun here to roust this newest bunch of owlhoots. So what happens then? Burke's sitting down here safe and sound, not breaking any laws. I tell you there's nothing we can do to him! Nothing we can do to stop—"

"Sue him," Prudence McKay said from the doorway.

Stark's head came up sharply. He hadn't seen her petite, feminine figure appear there. Behind her he spotted the pale tresses of Mindy Simmons. Prudence must've accompanied her to the office for her lunch date with Ronnie.

All three ranchers had swung about to stare at the intruders. Ronnie started to his feet at the sight of Mindy, but she waved him back.

"Fellows, let me present Miss Prudence McKay, attorney and counselor-at-law," Stark said as he rose. "Been my experience that it's usually worth listening to what she has to say about legal matters."

The ranchers had risen as well.

"Excuse me for interfering, gentlemen," Prudence apologized diplomatically. "I was in the outer office with Miss Simmons, and I couldn't help overhearing. Since I have some knowledge of the case from Mr. Stark, I ventured a suggestion. If I'm intruding then I'll withdraw."

"No. please stay," Bishop said quickly.

"What do you mean, sue him?" Hollingshed demanded. "Burke hasn't broken any laws here in the territory."

Prucence smiled slightly. "No criminal laws, perhaps, at least that we know of, but he may have violated our civil statutes or case law, which would give you ground to sue him in civil court for damages."

"Let's hear about it," Bishop requested with growing interest.

Stark made the introductions and got them seated, except for Ronnie, who ended up in feverish whispered conversation with Mindy in a corner.

"You gentlemen may wish for Miss Simmons to join us," Prudence suggested. "She is possibly our best witness at this point."

Ronnie broke off their talk to draw a hesitant Mindy forward. He pulled his chair very close to hers as they joined the group. Back behind his desk, Stark observed the goings-on with musing eyes.

"Just what is your interest in this, Miss McKay?" Hollingshed demanded, skeptical as usual.

"The interest any attorney should have in seeing justice done, and in seeing to it that the law isn't manipulated by unscrupulous individuals for their own dishonest ends," she replied levelly. "Also, I'm a friend of Miss Simmons, and she has suffered indirectly at Burke's hands. I'm not soliciting business. I won't even charge you for my time today. You can take what I tell you, and do with it what you please."

"What law has Burke broken?" Bishop inquired before Hollingshed could frame a reply.

"It's called conversion. He may have converted

your property—that is, your livestock—for his own benefit.''

''Explain that a little further,'' Bishop encouraged.

''If someone wrongfully takes something you own and sells it or puts it to his own use in some other fashion, it's known legally as conversion. When that happens, you are entitled to damages for for your losses, even if, technically, no crime has been committed.''

''He took our livestock, all right, but he did it up in the Unassigned Lands where none of the courts have any jurisdiction,'' Hollingshed challenged.

Prudence nodded patiently. ''As I understand matters, he knowingly bought stolen livestock, sold it, and no doubt used the money for his own purposes.''

''But he did it up in no-man's-land,'' Hollingshed snapped impatiently.

Prudence smiled sweetly. ''Randall Burke isn't is in no-man's-land, and neither is his money or his other holdings. They're all right here in Oklahoma Territory, and under the jurisdiction of the courts here. We can't sue him in the Unassigned Lands, but we can certainly sue him here.''

Stark felt a tingle of growing excitement. The ranchers were mulling her words over. He tried to catch Prudence's eye and nod his encouragement. If she saw it, she didn't let on.

''And you're saying you can prove this in court?'' Hollingshed wasn't convinced.

''I'm saying we can get Randall Burke into court,'' Prudence corrected. ''Whether we succeed in proving our case is another matter.''

"What good does it do to get him in court?"

"Because," Prudence said, "when he's in court, then he's in my territory."

All three of the ranchers stared at her. Even Hollingshed seemed impressed. Mindy's eyes had grown wide as she looked on.

"And you could handle this case for us?" Bishop queried.

"I could handle it," Prudence assured him.

Bishop swung his head toward Stark. "Mr. Stark, what's your thinking on this?"

"I already told you she's a fine attorney. For my money, I wouldn't have anyone else representing me."

Bishop nodded thoughtfully.

"That's good enough for me!" Ronnie chimed in.

"You'd be taking on a mighty powerful man, Miss McKay," Hollingshed pointed out.

"I've taken on powerful men before, Mr. Hollingshed." Prudence met his gaze coolly.

Hollingshed's eyes flicked away. "Just the same, you may want to bring some other lawyer on board to help you. Someone with a lot of experience—"

"I have a lot of experience, Mr. Hollingshed."

"Your experience might not be enough. We might need somebody else."

"We might need a man?" Prudence spoke without inflection. "Is that what you mean?"

"I just ain't had occasion to deal with very many lady lawyers, is all," Hollingshed said gruffly. "If having a lawyer who's a man would help us, then we ought to consider it."

"I work alone, gentlemen," Prudence addressed all three of them. "I'll take this particular case on a contingency fee basis. Those are my terms."

"You understand we need some time to discuss this, Miss McKay," Bishop temporized.

"Of course." Prudence smiled politely. "Take all the time you need."

"Fellows, I promised this pretty little gal here I'd escort her to lunch," Ronnie said, rising and beaming on Mindy. "And I reckon it's about lunchtime. I'll just catch up with you later for all this palaver."

With awkward gallantry he offered Mindy his arm.

She was blushing fit to kill. "Prudence, Jim, won't you join us?" Her words came out in a nervous rush.

"We'd be happy to," Prudence accepted her offer immediately.

Stark figured he wasn't going to have a say in the matter. But the prospect wasn't unpleasant.

The outer office was empty. Bishop and Hollingshed left, with Ronnie and Mindy in their wake.

"Thanks for the endorsement," Prudence said to Stark in passing as she went out the door.

Deftly Stark caught her elbow and wheeled her about back into the office. She let out a small gasp of surprise at finding herself almost in his arms.

Stark gave her a little room. "All that business about bringing suit against Burke sounded kind of personal to me," he accused.

She met his gaze innocently, tilting her head far back to look up at him. "I don't like having a man such as Randall Burke lie to me so that I make a fool of myself before a . . . a friend. And there's nothing wrong with an attorney taking a personal interest in winning a case.''

Stark cocked his head. ''Seems I recollect you singing a different tune when it came to me doing my job. Something about you objecting to personal vendettas, as I recall.''

He fancied a ghost of a smile brushed her lips, as at a fond memory, but she ducked her head before he could be sure. When she raised her face back up to him an instant later, he couldn't read her expression at all. ''I suppose a personal vendetta can be condoned now and again,'' she conceded in a husky voice, then placed both hands lightly against his chest, as if to hold him at bay. ''But I'm not your personal property, Jim Stark.''

Stark shifted his weight against the warmth of her palms and looked down square into her brown eyes. ''Yes, ma'am,'' he agreed solemnly.

''Just so that's understood.'' A spark of mischief danced in her gaze. ''Now, come on, we're keeping the youngsters waiting.'' She caught his arm and, with a deftness of her own, turned him smoothly out into the hallway.

Chapter Fourteen

"Any developments?" Stark asked as he entered the office.

Prudence looked up from the clutter of books and papers on her desk. In the light from the lamp by which she worked, Stark was struck suddenly by her beauty. He hadn't realized how much he'd missed her.

"Jim! I'm glad you're back!" Rising, she came quickly from behind her desk, then seemed to catch herself. Her smile was still radiant as she clasped one of his hands in both of hers and drew him to one of the upholstered client chairs. She settled into the other as he was seated.

"Told you I'd be back for the hearing," Stark reminded her. He'd been absent from Guthrie for a week on an investigation. Arriving by train in the gathering dusk, he had hoofed it straight to Prudence's law office on the hunch he might yet find her there.

She leaned back in her chair, and Stark saw the pull of tension in the smooth lines of her trim figure. "The hearing on my motion is still set for first thing tomorrow morning," she told him. "I spent all afternoon working on my supplemental brief so I could get it filed before the courthouse closed. I delivered the judge's copy to him personally. I want it to be the last pleading he sees before the hearing."

"Who's Burke's lawyer?"

"Millard Cranton."

"Shyster," Stark said dismissively.

"I agree," Prudence said with feeling. "Most of his clients are crooks or murderers, and he's about on a level with them. But he's slippery as an eel in court. I'm still preparing for oral arguments in the morning." She straightened a bit in the chair. "You'll be there, won't you?"

Stark nodded. "May be running a little late. I've got to go by the telegraph office and see if I've gotten responses to some things I was checking on." He pondered a moment. "You figure the judge will freeze Burke's assets like you requested in your motion?"

Prudence let her shoulders sag tiredly. "I don't know. I filed the motion mainly for nuisance value to keep the other side off balance, but I'm starting to hope we have a chance of actually winning. The judge has the power to grant our motion if he wants to, but it's certainly not normal procedure in a case like this. The judge needs to be convinced there's a real danger of Burke transferring his funds to another jurisdiction where the court can't reach them."

She chewed at her full lower lip for a moment, then sighed. "It almost means the judge has to decide this early in the case that Burke is as big of a scoundrel as we allege he is, and that's not too likely. Burke's got a solid reputation in Guthrie. For us to have a real chance I think we need some documentary evidence to support our allegations. But all we've got is the potential testimony of witnesses to link Burke to the wrongdoings in the Unassigned Lands. That may not be enough to get a freeze on his assets this early in the case.'' She gave a frustrated shake of her head.

Stark kept his own counsel. ''Have you had supper?'' he asked to change the subject.

''Heavens, is it that late?'' Prudence rose up enough to look out the window behind her chair. ''I suppose it is,'' she concluded. She drew a palm across her face. ''Supper sounds wonderful,'' she said with a rueful smile. ''But I really need to finish preparing for the hearing. I think I'll just take my file back to my room and have something sent up for dinner.''

Stark was surprised at his disappointment. ''I'll walk you to your hotel,'' he offered.

Her smile was bright. ''I'd like that.''

Stark watched as she bustled about the desk with renewed vigor. ''Ready,'' she announced at last.

With Stark toting her oversize briefcase, they left her office. She took his arm and actually hummed a little bit as they strolled through the cool autumn air. Shuttered carriages clattered past on the cobblestones. The street lamps were just being lit.

''Any word from the lovebirds?'' Stark inquired dryly.

She gave a muffled giggle. ''They arrived this afternoon and are staying at my hotel. Ronnie finally saved up enough to get her an engagement ring, and she's walking on air. He is too, for that matter.''

''Have they set a date to jump the broomstick?''

Reflexively, it seemed, her fingers tightened momentarily on his bicep. ''They don't want to wait until spring. They've set it for the day after Thanksgiving. We're invited.''

When Ronnie had returned to his ranch after the decision had been reached to hire Prudence, he had taken Mindy with him. The last Stark had heard, she had been living and working as a seamstress in a nearby community while Ronnie scrimped and saved on his ranch for the caliber of ring he thought she deserved. Ronnie was to be the stockmen's representative at tomorrow's hearing.

Turning his head, Stark peered hard into the gloom of an alley's mouth as he and Prudence passed.

She must've felt the tension in his arm. "What's wrong?"

"Just habit," Stark brushed her query aside.

"You're afraid Burke might be lying in wait for us," she said with disturbing perception.

Stark hitched his shoulders. "It's a thought."

Prudence shook her head soberly. "He won't risk breaking the law at this juncture. He can't afford to have some henchman who might implicate him brought up on criminal charges."

"No, he can't, can he?" Stark muttered thoughtfully.

At her door she turned and smiled up at him, reaching to take the valise from his grip. Their hands brushed. Her shoulder drooped under the weight of the case. "Good night," she said.

He felt once again that soft, restraining touch of her palm on his chest. He fancied that her hand trembled. Then she slipped quickly through her doorway and was gone.

Stark left the hotel with a host of notions and impressions jumbled in his mind. As he headed down shadowed sidestreets toward his own lodgings, he felt the hairs rise at the nape of his neck. Smoothly, as a continuation of his stride, he pivoted, brushing the tail of his coat back from the butt of the .45. He saw only the slightest hint of movement at the edge of the pool of light cast by a distant street lamp. It could've been only his imagination. The sensation of being watched faded.

Warily he continued on to his hostelry. Burke looked to have been lying low, he mused, apparently content to let his shady mouthpiece do his talking for him in court. And Prudence was right; it would be a fool's move for Burke to resort to violence with the court case only in its early stages. Still, someone had sure been skulking on his backtrail, whether as an agent of Burke of some other enemy, he didn't know. In any event, he concluded darkly, it would pay to tread carefully from here on out.

At the telegraph office the next morning, he stood for a long time studying the fistful of wires he had received. Some of them were long enough to have raised the ire of whatever luckless operator had taken them down.

Satisfied at last, the suspicion of a grin drawing at his mouth, he stuffed the missives into his coat pocket and ankled swiftly to the courthouse. The hearing was already under way, he realized as he mounted the stairs.

In the rough-and-tumble world of Oklahoma Territory law, the federal judges were given a lot of leeway in administering the statutes, most of which had been lifted from Kansas or other neighboring states. Even so, Stark knew, Prudence had an uphill battle in front of her today.

But maybe he could level the ground a bit.

Millard Cranton, Burke's mouthpiece, had apparently asked for and received permission to address the court first. It was a violation of procedure on Prudence's motion, which didn't bode well for her chances of a favorable ruling.

Sweaty, fat as a hog, and clad in a tight, food-stained suit that showed every bulge of lard on his body, Burke's attorney nevertheless had the skilled, persuasive voice of an orator. From where he bulked large behind the lectern, his stentorian tones rolled and reverberated commandingly in the crowded courtroom. The case had attracted some attention among local wags and reporters. There were plenty of onlookers to the proceedings.

Chief Justice Edward B. Green sported a curly, rectangular white beard. His receding ridge of thick snowy hair stood out in sharp contrast to his black robe. His long face was fixed in attentive listening.

''My client is an honorable, law-abiding citizen of this community, Your Honor,'' Cranton proclaimed. ''You yourself have dined in his fine restaurant. He has no black marks to besmirch his name or reputation, save the scandalous and patently false allegations made by this young woman and her cohorts, who are not even citizens of the territory!''

Doffing his Stetson, Stark made his way down the aisle and through the swinging gate in the waist-high divider to join Prudence and Ronnie Hall at her counsel table before the bench. He noted Mindy's pale blond head in the front row of the public pews as he passed.

Dressed stiffly in his Sunday-go-to-meeting best, Ronnie still looked ready for a scrap, but was managing to restrain himself. Stark took a seat at the single chair remaining beside Ronnie. Prudence glanced about at him, barely seeming to notice his arrival. Her pretty face was drawn in fierce concentration. Plenty of notes were scribbled on the pad in front of her. She knew she was being outmaneuvered, and she wouldn't have liked the reference to her age or sex. She looked ready for a scrap herself.

Stark glanced the width of the courtroom. Seated at the other counsel table, Randall Burke appeared big and prosperous and confident. He gave a contemptuous shake of his head as he saw Stark.

In the chair beyond him, nearest the wall, was the impassive figure of Chin. The Chinese killer, Stark reflected, would have the hunter's skill needed to move in the darkness like the menacing shadow he had glimpsed the night before.

"I can find no precedent for what this little lady is requesting be done to my client," Cranton boomed. "It is unconscionable that such a thing should even be considered. Putting a freeze on his assets would only prevent him from carrying on his business, which, I might point out, provides many benefits to this community, besides the fine food and entertainment it offers!"

Stark figured Cranton was no stranger to either of those two commodities, especially when it came to stuffing his belly. He knew objections were generally out of order at this stage of the proceedings, but he could tell Prudence was near the point of trying one anyway.

Stark pulled the telegrams from his pocket, smoothed them out on the table, then handed them to Ronnie to pass on to Prudence. The wrangler complied. When Prudence glanced sharply about at Stark, he winked.

She set to perusing the documents. After a minute or so, Stark saw her shoulders square up beneath the padded fabric of her dark dress. She shot him a single wide-eyed look, then put all her attention back on the missives.

She completed her review within minutes. Rising unobtrusively, she rounded Ronnie's chair and bent close to Stark. He caught the sweet smell of some scent she wore. Her face was only inches from his.

"Where did you get these?" she demanded in a soft whisper.

"I checked with some contacts I have through the Pinkertons back East," he advised sotto voce. "They're the real McCoy. Backup documents are on the way."

Prucence smiled like a cat. "That's all I needed to know." She slipped back to her chair.

"I have nothing else, Ed, I mean, Your Honor." Cranton was winding down at last. "I reckon we can let this young lady say a few words, although maybe after this she'll confine her work to the kitchen where she belongs!"

A chorus of laughter rippled through the mostly male audience. Stark stiffened, then made himself settle down. As Prudence had said, this was her territory. Let her do whatever fighting needed to be done.

Prudence ignored the laughter. As Cranton waddled and heaved his way back to his chair, she rose, her notepad and the telegrams in hand, and moved deliberately to the podium. The laughter was fading away, to be replaced by a hum of conversation. It didn't diminish when she took her place behind the lectern. Prudence ignored that as well. She didn't hurry in arranging the papers in front of her. Then, not even bothering to look up, she began to review them carefully.

After a handful of seconds, the judge banged his gavel down and growled for order. The talk among the spectators died away.

For the first time Prudence lifted her head. Stark felt a surge of pride. Without saying a word, she had established her authority in the room.

"Your Honor," she began in a crisp, carrying voice, "I won't list the improprieties which have already taken place here this morning. I'm sure you are fully aware of each of them. I will say, however, that, although I have not been spending much time in the kitchen, from the looks of my honorable opposing counsel, someone has certainly been spending a good deal of time there working on his behalf."

It was a moment before her words sank in. Then a man guffawed, and the laughter rolled through the courtroom. Even the judge's bearded face cracked a tight grin at Cranton's expense. Only the trio at the other counsel table didn't look amused by the remark.

"May it please the Court," Prudence went on as the laughter waned, "my investigator, James Stark, has uncovered evidence which will conclusively show that the Defendant, Mr. Burke, is heavily indebted to certain illegal and illicit enterprises operating out of New York and other eastern cities. His finances are in such precarious condition that he cannot afford to lose a lawsuit here in Oklahoma Territory, and, rather than risk it, he will undoubtedly attempt to transfer his funds back East or elsewhere to shelter them.''

Sputtering, Cranton heaved to his feet. ''I object! This is highly improper!''

''As was much of what you said and did in your oral argument, Counselor,'' Prudence retorted with barely a glance at him.

The judge was frowning. ''Go on, Miss McKay,'' he directed. ''I'll hear a little more of what you have to say, at any rate.''

''Thank you.'' Prudence lifted the sheaf of telegrams. ''I have here telegrams, soon to be documented by sworn affidavits, legal records, and financial statements from various law enforcement and detective agencies, confirming that Mr. Burke has borrowed money from at least two crime families who operate most of the gambling, dope, and prostitution activities in New York, as well as from a Chinese tong in that city.''

Stark knew the presence of Burke's pet Chinese killer would make that last allegation ring true with most folks hereabouts.

Apparently it did with Judge Green. ''Let me see those telegrams, Miss McKay.'' As she left the podium, he glanced toward the other counsel table. ''You may approach also, Mr. Cranton.''

The corpulent attorney broke off a fierce whispered discussion with his client to heave up out of his chair. He lumbered to the bench, towering hugely beside Prudence's tiny figure. She edged a little bit away from his coarse bulk.

The judge examined the wire messages one at a time, passing each of them to Cranton as he finished. Prudence made no objection. Cranton seemed mighty interested in the documents, Stark noted. Could be, he was learning a few things he didn't know about his own client.

"And just what parties do you represent, Miss McKay?" the judge asked when he handed the final sheet to Cranton.

"Ranchers in the Indian Lands, Your Honor; good men; salt of the earth." She named them. Stark fancied he saw the judge's eyes flicker in recognition at a couple of the names.

"These are all slanderous forgeries, Your Honor!" Cranton asserted, laying the last sheet aside. His booming voice had lost some of its timbre.

The judge ignored him. "You say you can document these matters?" he asked, addressing Prudence. "If so, how long will it take?"

"Yes, sir, we can," she said with utter confidence. "Two weeks will be sufficient."

The judge looked thoughtfully to Cranton. "Counselor, do you have anything to add?"

Cranton licked fleshy lips. "With all due respect, the Court has no authority to freeze my client's assets," he began in protest.

"Your objections are noted." The judge cut him

off. "You're free to appeal my ruling if you don't like it. The federal government has placed a great deal of power in the hands of the judiciary here in Oklahoma Territory. I allow some freedom in my courtroom when it comes to procedures, but I view the role of the Court as protecting this territory. I have been called a friend of the masses. I hope that is true. We are just now on the verge of turning the tide against the lawless element which has held sway in these parts for some time. I will not be a party, directly or indirectly, to opening the gate to the more insidious criminal elements from back East. I am from Illinois. There are similar organized criminal establishments in Chicago. So far, thank God, the territory is clear of the type of criminal operations with which your client has apparently allied himself. To give them a foothold here would be, *sui generis,* a travesty of justice."

He raised a hand to forestall a further objection from Cranton. "I am not deciding this lawsuit in favor of Miss McKay's clients. That may or may not come later when all the evidence is in. But I am ordering your client, Randall Burke, not to attempt to remove or transfer any of his assets or property out of the jurisdiction of this court for a period of two weeks. He may continue to operate his business interests hereabouts. If, as you claim, these allegations prove groundless, your client will only have been inconvenienced for a brief period. And I will entertain a motion to hold Miss McKay's clients liable for damages he may have suffered." He banged his gavel down. "Plaintiff's motion is granted. Bailiff, call the next case on my docket."

''Whoo-ee!'' Ronnie cut loose once they were out of the courthouse. ''I reckon you showed that tub of lard, Miss McKay! Tarnation, but you're a scrapper in court!''

Prudence flashed a brilliant smile at Stark. ''I couldn't have done it without my trusted investigator,'' she quipped, then sobered a bit. ''You can provide the documentation I promised, can't you?''

''It's on its way,'' Stark promised.

''So we've won!'' Ronnie slipped an arm around Mindy's shoulders and gave her a quick hug to her immense embarrassment.

''Not in public, Ronnie!'' she chided, but her face was radiant.

''We've just won the first battle,'' Prudence cautioned.

''Maybe we've won more than that,'' Stark said. ''I've also learned that Burke is behind in his payments to those Eastern outfits. I don't know what he's done with his money. Maybe he's sunk it into his rustling operation. But he hasn't kept up on what he owes his lenders, and those boys don't take kindly to bad debts. They'll get word of this, and they'll be looking for their money, one way or the other.'' He broke off without saying more.

''Jim!'' Prudence demanded with that uncanny perception. ''What are you planning?''

''Let's just say I'm going to do a little more investigating,'' Stark told her.

Chapter Fifteen

Stark sauntered once more into the fancy gaming
room of the Golden Apple. He moved to the far end
of the bar where he could have his back to the wall.
The patrons there made room for him. He felt their
curious eyes on him as he ordered his usual beer. More
than one noted the sheathed bowie knife riding his belt
along with the namesake .45. In spite of the coolness
outdoors, he wore no coat.

The place was busy tonight. Word had spread of
what had happened in court that morning, but it didn't
seem to have bothered business much, Stark mused
wryly. The gaming tables were crowded. Roulette
balls clattered. The voices of the house dealers seemed
a little louder than usual. The players shifted restlessly
from game to game. Wins were greeted with cheers
from onlookers; losses were heartily condemned.
Pretty girls, and a few ladies, were scattered about in
the crowd. Their voices and laughter rose shrilly. A
sharp sense of tension hung over the big room, almost
as tangible as the fumes of whiskey and tobacco.

Burke himself was nowhere in sight. Probably lick-
ing his wounds, Stark concluded with satisfaction. His
investigations into Burke's background had unearthed
more than he'd expected. Burke was a powerful, dan-

gerous man, but he'd picked some pards who were mighty dangerous themselves when crossed. After today's court ruling, Burke would be starting to feel desperate. Ugly collection methods might already be under way. The restaurant owner was likely to be close to the edge of the law himself.

Stark saw no sign, either, of Burke's deadly bodyguard. He narrowed his eyes to focus on the far wall and caught the gleam of metal. The coin was still embedded there. He smiled thinly. Chin's trophy of his victory over the Peacemaker. The wager had become the stuff of local legend.

"You got a heap of nerve sashaying in here tonight," a rugged bartender at Stark's elbow commented without heat.

"That a fact?" Stark answered noncommittally.

The fellow nodded. "The boss has been on the warpath ever since he got back from court this morning. I hear that lady lawyer worked him over with a bullwhip." He didn't sound too displeased at the thought.

"That's close enough to what happened," Stark said and grinned.

The bartender seemed about to say something further, then shrugged and glanced furtively about. "Watch your back around here," he muttered as he turned away.

Sympathetic or not, Stark knew the barkeep would report his presence to Burke. The nape-prickling sensation of being watched touched him. A pretty young woman with a modest dress and golden curls appeared out of the crowd almost at his side. She gave him a hesitant smile and eased up to the bar to order sarsaparilla. The bartender made no comment as he complied.

It looked like Burke might already be aware of him, Stark reflected. The blond sipped decorously, caught his eye as if by accident, and shook her curls ruefully. "My beau's luck is all bad tonight," she told him.

Only the way she moved, and the blue ice deep down in her eyes, gave her away for what she was. Her beau would be whoever happened to be the biggest winner at the moment, and for a price she could be part of the winnings. Just another service offered by Randall Burke. She was bait for every hombre in the place, including himself, Stark knew. But in his case, the trap she baited was likely to be deadly. He smiled grimly at the thought, and she shrank back from him a bit.

She would just get in the way, and be a danger to him besides. He jerked his head in wordless dismissal. Frowning, she retreated into the crowd. Stark put an extra coin on the bar for the barkeep, and drifted out into the night. He'd shown himself long enough.

He killed a little more time at the notorious Blue Bell Saloon nearby. Then, nerves taut, he headed west toward Coffee Creek and the more disreputable section of town, choosing a darkened street where the glow from the lamps reached only dimly. He let the heels of his boots clatter on the cobblestones underfoot.

The slight, gun-hung figure seemed to take form out of the gloom some twenty paces ahead of him.

"Stark! You pulled a trick draw on me before. It won't happen again! You hear me?"

Stark recognized the high-pitched tones of Stace,

the trigger-happy kid who'd been one of the trio roughing up Ronnie the night the affair had begun. Alarm throbbed through Stark's muscles, because this wasn't the way it was supposed to work. Stace knew there hadn't been any trick draw. He knew Stark had beaten him, and had let him live only out of the goodness of his heart. Not even Stace would be fool enough to challenge him straight up again.

''Well, Peacemaker?'' Stace's sharp tones bounced from the shabby buildings lining the street.

Stark's eyes cut one way, then the other, to the alley mouth on his left, and to the false-fronted two-story building on his right. He understood then. Maybe he should've stayed at the Golden Apple after all. Bait or no, it might've been been a better setup than this.

There was no point in giving them any more time. ''Make your play, cowboy!'' Stark called, and drew.

He pulled the Colt with a sweeping movement of his hand. As he fired, he dropped and rolled sideward like a log—another draw he hadn't shown Ronnie, one he didn't even know if he could make himself. There was no aiming; he could rely only on the reflex and instinct of his gun hand. He triggered once as he fell. Flame stabbed back at him from Stace's scrawny figure. Stark rolled and fired again. Stace hollered in pain and shock.

A rifle cracked from the rooftop on his right. The bullet screamed off the cobblestones by Stark's ear. Another six-gun opened up on him from the alley mouth. Stace had only been the distraction. Now he was under three guns.

He flung lead in the direction of the alley, twisted

up on one knee and triggered at the hunched form just showing above the top of the false front on the building. From his yell, Stace had been hit and hit hard. Stark didn't have time to fret about him. Bullets ripped the night about him, chipping the street inches from where he crouched. He'd thrown their aims by his movement. He couldn't afford to let his own be thrown off.

The gunman in the alley was shooting wild, just cocking the hammer and pulling the trigger. The rifleman on the roof was the dangerous one. Right-handed, Stark fired the Colt at his hunched figure, punching at least one shot through the flimsy wood of the façade behind which he crouched. Even as he was shooting, he whipped the double-action Marlin .38 from the holster at his spine. Not looking around, firing blind, he thrust it in the direction of the alley and pulled the trigger again and again.

The bulky figure atop the roof lurched upright, the shape of the rifle clenched in outthrust fists. Stark thought it was the shot through the façade that had scored. He put the last round of the .45 square in the center of the silhouetted form, and saw the bushwhacker fold over the edge of the façade. Rifle and all, he plummeted headlong to the hard cobblestones.

The firing from the alley's mouth had stopped. Stark doubted if his own blind return fire had hit anything. Maybe the sight of his victim shooting back without looking had unnerved the gunman. A choking cloud of powdersmoke enveloped Stark as he rose. His ears screamed like banshees in the aftermath of the gunfire.

With a quick rush he gained the alley, positioning

himself just to one side of its mouth. He dropped the Colt back into its holster and shifted the Marlin to his right hand. The smaller gun still had a couple of loads left.

Breathing tightly, he forced himself to ignore the keening in his ears. From back in the alley came the pant of harsh breathing and the scrabble of frantic, booted feet. A faint gleam of reflection at Stark's foot caught his eye. He cocked his head and made out the shape of a revolver. Out of bullets, or panicked, or both, the last ambusher had dropped his gun. And from the sounds of it, he'd run into a dead end in the alley.

Like a shadow himself, Stark slipped into the gloom. He kept the .38 ready. Like him, the bushwhacker might be packing two guns. He paced forward, placing his feet carefully to avoid the trash and debris littering the ground. Ahead, he saw that the passage ended in a tall board fence. Light from a street lamp somewhere beyond cast a pale fan of illumination over the fence and the hombre trying to scale it.

''Box canyon,'' Stark said out of the darkness. ''No way out.''

The bushwhacker whirled with the litheness of a cornered puma. His teeth were gritted in a snarl. A long-bladed fighting knife served him just fine in place of talons. Stace's recognized the knife as well as the face. Here was Stace's other pard, who had pulled the same blade on Stark in their first fracas.

The rowdy froze at sight of the .38, but there was no fear evident in him now, only a demon's savagery. Maybe he was no great shakes when it came to having the nerve to throw down on a man from ambush. But cornered, with his knife in his hand, he looked tough and capable and ready for trouble.

Stark stilled the automatic flex of his trigger finger. He didn't know how the other two drygulchers had fared, but this one was still alive for certain, and Stark wanted him kept that way.

The hardcase read a chance in Stark's hesitation. ''You're packing that bowie of yours this time, Peacemaker,'' he challenged. ''You as good with it as they say?''

''Didn't need it last time,'' Stark reminded him. But the .38 disappeared and the bowie flashed suddenly in the pale light. The brass inlay gleamed like gold.

''Yeah,'' the hardcase breathed in wicked satisfaction, and came at him.

He was a slasher, sweeping and slicing his blade through the air in a bewildering web of steel. In theory, it left him open to the straight thrusts and lunges Stark fancied. But he swung the heavy blade with enough power to sever tendons and chop into bone if a counterthrust was misjudged or too slow. And Stark wanted him alive. Crossing blades with a man you weren't looking to kill was asking for a hard time.

And Stark found this one plenty hard. The slashing blade hewed and cut across and back and up and down too fast for him to be sure of a disabling attack in return. Stark slid away, circling to stay within the lighted area. Tangling with this character in the gloom behind him in the alley was a mistake he didn't figure to make.

The blade slashed in an odd backhanded uppercut

at Stark's gut. Stark thrust the bowie down, twisting his wrist. Steel chimed on steel as the uppercut was turned aside. Stark leaned the rest of the way into a lunge. The hardcase cursed and sprang clear. He'd been cut on his side. It wasn't serious, but no doubt it told him that the Peacemaker's rep was for real. He cursed again and came back in his slashing attack.

With speed, strength, and endurance a slasher could sometimes best a man who favored the lunge and the thrust. This hombre had all three. For a moment Stark was hemmed against the fence. Now he was the one in the box canyon, and his foes's knife seemed to be everywhere at once, shining in the lamplight, flashing at his eyes, cutting at his midriff, chopping down at his neck.

Strike for strike he parried, and they danced to the music of cold steel. Stark's eyes read the hewing angles and anticipated the slashing arcs, and his arm snaked, hooked, and turned to meet steel with steel. More than once he felt the impact of the other's blade against the fighting hilt of the bowie, and savvied it was the only thing that saved his fingers, and his life.

But he savvied also that even the best slashers were given to patterns, and, at last, as his shoulder began to ache with the speed and strength of his shifting parries, he caught a pattern to his opponent's moves. Left to right in a slash at his middle, returning in a blur from the other direction, then twisting to come up in that odd backhanded uppercut that could carve him like a turkey if he let it.

Scant inches in front of his belly, Stark brought the bowie down to intercept the uprising cut. In the last instant he rotated the bowie so that it was the brass inlay along its back that met the edge of the slasher's cut. Keen steel bit into soft brass, and wedged. Stark bore down hard before his foe could wrench loose.

As fast as his knife hand, Stark's left pistoned out in three driving jabs between the hardcase's eyes. The punishing blows staggered the smaller man. Stark felt the other's hold on his hilt loosen. He twisted violently with his right, and the slasher's blade went spinning away into the darkness. Stark's arm came up and around over his head in a circle. He hammered the hilt of the bowie down to the juncture of neck and shoulder. The hardcase sagged to his knees like a sack of potatoes, not out, but helpless beneath the numbing stroke.

Stark stepped back. ''As good as they say,'' he said gratingly. He ran his thumb over the new gash in the brass. Now there was another one in the collection.

He hauled the slasher roughly to his feet and poked him with the tip of the bowie. ''Head on back to the street.''

The rowdy didn't give him any trouble. The whole affair, from when Stace had first challenged him, had only taken a handful of minutes. There were shouted voices drawing nearer the gloomy street, but no one had yet pegged it as the source of the gunfire.

Stark prodded his prisoner to the fallen rifleman. It was, as Stark had suspected, the burly member of the trio he'd dropped with a flying kick to protect Ronnie. Something—maybe a fistful of greenbacks, or the relative safety of striking from ambush—had made him change his mind about tangling with the Peacemaker.

It had been a mistake. He was still alive, but in bad shape from the sound of his breathing.

The voices were getting closer. Stark marched his captive to the fallen Stace. The kid who'd been looking to gain a rep with his six-shooter had ended up gaining his bed of dirt after all.

The slasher kept his hand pressed to the wound at his side. ''I should've known we were fools for trying to take the Peacemaker,'' he said and groaned as he looked down at his fallen pard.

''Why did you try?'' Stark asked tersely.

The rowdy shook his head stubbornly. ''I need a doc,'' he complained.

''And I need answers.'' Stark's tone was cold.

The prisoner glanced hopefully in the direction of the approaching voices.

''They won't help you.''

The slasher's shoulders sank in defeat. ''Okay, I'll tell you. But first, how in blazes did you outshoot all three of us?''

''Grace of God,'' Stark said.

''You were expecting us, weren't you?'' the prisoner probed.

''You or somebody like you,'' Stark confirmed.

The slasher shook his head again, this time in resignation. ''When do I get to see a sawbones?''

''After you talk. And after we see the U.S. Marshal.''

Chapter Sixteen

"Where's your boss?" Stark growled.

The rugged barkeep eyed him curiously. "He's been around here talking to the customers. Don't see him at the moment, howsomever."

So Burke had been letting himself be seen, no doubt so he'd have an alibi, Stark mused grimly. "Where's his office?" he demanded.

Frowning, the barkeep jerked his head toward a polished door in the rear wall. "In back."

"Obliged."

Stark turned away and ran his gaze over the room. The tension was drawn even tighter than it had been on his first visit earlier in the evening. A few folks had noticed his entrance. Most were too intent on their games. Stark saw the blond bar girl. She had a new beau.

Stark started toward the door the barkeep had indicated. He'd taken two steps when it opened and a tall, lithe figure in a shabby, ill-fitting suit came into view. Behind him, Stark heard the bartender mutter an oath.

For the first time, Chin was alone. With a gliding step he came forward, and something in the coiled tightness of his walk made even the jaded gamesters pull back out of his way. His face could've been a mask cut from leather.

Someone saw Stark near the bar, and his name ran across the room in muffled whispers. More people shifted, and in a moment a passage had opened between him and Chin. Down its length, looking neither to his right nor his left, Chin came in his flowing stride. Stark stood waiting, his arms held loosely at his sides. Gradually the mumble of voices, the clatter of games, the clink of glasses faded. The tension stretched as taut as a drawn string on a bow.

Chin halted twenty feet from Stark and crossed his arms on his chest. He didn't speak. His eyes were oblong black slits in the mask of his face.

"I'm looking for Burke," Stark's voice rang out in the still room.

"He busy."

"Reckon I'll see him anyway."

"He not see you." Chin's tone was flat, as emotionless as his face.

"Guess we'll find out."

Stark did no more than shift his weight as though to advance, but Chin's arms whipped from across his chest. One arced back, then forward. The throwing ax he'd conjured from beneath his coat spun through the air at Stark so fast it sounded like a windmill in a high wind.

Stark did some conjuring himself. The Colt .45 that appeared in his fist tilted up and spat flame. Even above the roar of the shot came the shrill keen of lead on steel. Deflected by the bullet, the ax caromed to the side and buried itself in the mahogany rim of a pool table. Arm cocked, second ax poised to throw, Chin went rigid as an oak tree. The black slits of his eyes, staring down the smoking barrel of Stark's Colt, had gone a little wide.

Stark twitched the barrel of the pistol. "Drop it."

Chin's arm came down with the jerky movements of a wind-up toy. The ax clattered to the floor. Stark twitched the Colt again. Understanding, Chin kicked the fallen weapon aside with a hooking swipe of his foot. Face still impassive, he faced Stark.

Left-handed, Stark thumbed five gold pieces, one by one, onto the bar. "I figure Burke will cover that," he said. From the edge of his vision, he saw the barkeep grin.

Deliberately Stark doffed his Stetson and tossed it aside. Then he eased down the hammer on the .45 and slid it snugly back into its holster.

"Okay," he said to Chin. "Let's see how your parlor tricks work now."

For a span of seconds, Chin stood without understanding. Stark moved away from the bar in a smooth, gliding movement of his own, his fists lifting.

Then at last an expression creased Chin's face. He smiled. "Yes," he hissed with satisfaction. "This is as should be between warriors."

He shed his coat and flicked it away like a dark ghost. The straps that had held the axes crisscrossed his chest. Lifting one vertical open hand in front of his face, palm edge out, he pressed his other fist against his palm and bowed slightly.

Stark acknowledged the formality with a curt nod. Once again his reputation demanded a showdown, especially against a man who'd been publicly seen to best him. He'd worked too hard, taken too many lives, to let his name be linked to defeat.

But even more than his rep, his own reckoning of himself as a man demanded that Chin be brought down on his own terms. Even Stark's life was worth the risk. And, in a sense, it was more in danger here than in any face-off with a gun boss and his crew, because Stark was used to going up against gunmen, but only rarely did he face a man trained in anything like the sort of unarmed fighting skills he himself had.

And never had he faced one as deadly as Chin.

Fists up like a prizefighter, Stark coasted forward, weaving a little at the waist, up on his toes. Chin moved sidewise, one leg crossing over the other. He drew his open, curling hands in fancy circular movements in front of him. Air came from his mouth in a faint hiss. He drew fresh breath through nostrils that flared wide. He cocked his head ever so slightly.

Stark knew the Chinese type of empty-hand fighting had used movements of animals—crane, tiger, mantis, even the mythical dragon—to develop attacks and counters with feet and hands. He saw some of that now in Chin's graceful motions.

He didn't let what he didn't know about Chin's style worry him. Come right down to it, all ways of fighting that used kicks and punches in combinations had a lot in common, so much so that, when in action, it was sometimes hard to tell them apart. He wondered remotely if Chin knew beans about *savate*. The French art combined English-style pugilism with older European kicking techniques.

Still moving sideward, hands floating up and down, Chin edged toward him. The patrons of the gambling hall had drawn back to give them room, forming an arena bordered by avid, eager faces.

"Three to one on the Peacemaker!" a man's voice called.

As though it was a signal, Chin hopped closer and snapped his heavy shod foot at Stark's knee. Stark saw it would fall short. It was a feint. Chin's foot came down solidly on the hardwood floor, and he wheeled; his rear leg coming around, heelfirst, at Stark's ribs. Stark leaned clear. He dropped a cupped hand to catch Chin's extended ankle and propel him on all the way around in his spin. For a fleeting moment they were almost face-to-face.

Stark's knee hinged out. The toe of his boot drove at Chin's middle. Chin brought up his knee to muffle the kick. Then, like a cat, he raked the taloned fingers of one hand after the other at Stark's eyes. Stark had a glimpse of Chin's face alight with the savagery of combat. He raised up his fists like a boxer's to block the clawing attack, then jabbed with his left and followed it with a right straight from the shoulder. Both hit only air as Chin slid back.

Stark felt a stinging on his wrists. and realized that first blood had been drawn. It was trickling down his arms. Chin's fingernails had flayed his flesh. This Chinese type of fighting was bad medicine. He didn't like to think about what those fingers would've done to his face.

He moved in, jabbing with his left to set up the kick he drove out from his side. Following it, he spun and

mule-kicked, stretching his leg high, aiming his boot
to meet Chin's jaw. The iron heel of a palm chopped
his side kick down; a bent wrist banged his second
kick up high.

And Chin was after him like an avalanche of feet.
Kicks flew at him from every which direction, and
every which angle. Stark could only thrust his fists in
front of his face, tuck his elbows against his body, and
backpeddle before the assault. Chin's heavy clodhopper shoes thudded bruisingly against his arms, came
down stingingly on his knuckles, sent pain tingling
through his funny bone.

He was driven all the way to the bar. It's rail bit
into his spine. Chin pressed close, switching from feet
to hands. If anything, that made it worse. The taloned
fingers tore again at Stark's forearms. A stiffened hand
stabbed at his belly like an Indian lance. The edge of
a fist hammered on the top of his head and seemed to
jam his neck down between his shoulders. His knees
buckled.

Then the butt of Chin's driving palm took him
square in the breastbone. Stark felt like his heart had
been yanked to a brutal halt. Pain ripped up and down
and back and forth across his ribcage. Through tear-
blurred eyes he caught a glimpse of Randall Burke
standing in the forefront of the spectators. Burke had
ventured out of hiding, Stark understood dimly. And
he was gambling again, betting that, with Stark out of
the way, he could weather the ranchers' lawsuit and
his own failing finances. It was a good bet. Even now
Burke might walk away scot-free.

The thought goaded Stark like spurs. He braced

himself and hooked his fists, right and left, into Chin's body, twisting the blows as he struck, repeating the sequence again and then again, with his shoulders behind every blow. Chin's slashing, pounding hands weakened. Stark straightened his knees as he uppercut with his right fist. The blow drove Chin's head far back on a neck that bent like India rubber.

Chin skipped away to regain his balance. For an instant he poised like some great wading bird on one leg, uplifted foot spearing out in short, stabbing drives. Stark brushed the kicks aside, stamped at the knee of Chin's anchor leg. Shifting weight and balance, he stiffened his other leg to shove his foot like a battering ram into Chin's midriff.

The force of the thrust drove the warrior flailing into the arms of the crowd. They gave like the ropes of a prizefight ring. A dozen willing hands shoved Chin back into the fray. He took advantage of the momentum, adding the driving strength of his own legs. With a caterwauling screech from down in his gut, he flung himself into the air, lead foot flashing out.

Stark twisted aside. Chin's driving foot met the three-inch bar rail and cracked it clean as a stick of kindling. Stark crouched and sprang atop the bar. As Chin recovered from his leaping attack, Stark shifted his boots on the polished mahogany and kicked at Chin's head. The height should've given him an advantage.

It didn't. Chin leaned away from the kick and twirled his body in a spinning arc. Like a scythe, one upraised leg swept around to cut Stark's feet full from under him. He crashed down on the bar with a force that jolted his throbbing ribs and rattled the bottles and glasses in the rack behind him on the wall.

For an instant the pressed tin ceiling spun and tilted crazily in his vision. He barely spotted the heel of Chin's foot hammering down at his skull like a sledge. It was near the same type of kick Stark had used to smash the gaming table during the wager. Stark rolled his head aside, and Chin's descending heel smashed wood a scant inch from his face. Splinters dug into his flesh.

Even Chin had a little trouble getting his extended leg back under him. Twisting onto his side, Stark snapped a foot around in an arc. It nailed Chin just above the ear. There wasn't a lot of force behind it, but it sent Chin staggering back. Stark rolled off the bar.

His head was clearing now. But the air was beginning to rasp in his throat with each stabbing breath. His legs and reflexes, already strained taut by the earlier knife fight, were starting to play out. He had to force himself to go after his foe.

Chin surged to meet him, and they wheeled, spun, and leaped back and forth across the makeshift arena, with the crowd ebbing and flowing about them, and shouted bets being raised and lowered with each blow struck or missed.

Stark boxed, jabbing, crossing with his hard fists, then bringing his legs into play, once hopping into the air like a jackrabbit to unleash a kick that Chin swatted aside with a palm that bruised like a flung stone. Chin's own hands flashed and pounded and tore, and his feet flew like swooping hawks.

As he sidestepped a high, snapping kick, Stark glimpsed Ronnie Hall in the crowd. The wrangler yelled encouragement. Beside him, her face drawn and pale, was the slight, feminine form of Prudence Mc-Kay. Somehow she had found out what was happening, and now she was here, seeing what he hadn't wanted her to see.

Knowledge of her presence slowed Stark for a fractional moment. That gave Chin the chance he needed. His foot snapped in another high arc that caught Stark's jaw and slewed his head hard around. It rocked him, but he kept his feet under him, so he was able to see Chin spin into the familiar high whirling kick that had enabled him to embed a coin in the solid wall of the saloon.

Stark had been waiting for it, expecting it. He gathered himself and sprang, his body a mirror image of Chin's. Both men's feet snapped out. Their attack yells sounded together, Stark's ringing louder. In midair their legs crossed like drawn swords, and it was Stark's boot that drove deep into Chin's body and doubled him like a jackknife. Chin crashed to the floor in a huddled heap.

Panting, Stark stood over him. He was still alert for a flicking hand or foot. But Chin was finished. It showed in the dying flame of the eyes that gazed up at Stark in wonder.

"The wager," Chin gasped. "You could've won!"

"It was a sucker's bet," Stark said expressionlessly. "I wanted to see what you could do. No reason to let you know what I could do."

Chin's mouth quirked in a bleak smile of understanding. "At least," he managed. "I die at the hands of a warrior."

"Yes," Stark answered.

The flame in the dark eyes flickered out.

The ranks of spectators were silent. On legs that didn't want to be steady, Stark wheeled away from his fallen opponent. The rising murmur of voices died as the onlookers saw where he was headed. Randall Burke squared his broad shoulders and stood his ground. He was still on his own turf, still in charge.

"That's a hundred o' gold you owe me." Stark gestured at Chin.

Burke ignored the remark. "You've got a lot to answer for, Stark."

"So do you. Difference is, you'll be doing it in jail. I'm taking you in."

Burke gave a snort of laughter. "Big talk," he said sneeringly. "You got no authority to arrest me. There's no law backing you."

Left-handed, Stark palmed the six-pointed silver star from under his gun belt. "Here's my law," he said coolly. "This means I'm a special Deputy U.S. Marshal. Evett Nix appointed me just a little bit earlier this evening when I took your hired gun to jail. He's over there right now, spilling his guts about how you paid him and his pards to bushwhack me. That's against the law, Burke—attempted murder. You ain't operating in no-man's-land now. I'm placing you under arrest. Nix has a cell waiting. You coming peaceable or not?"

Stricken, Burke stared. He read the truth in Stark's flat, unyielding gaze. His own eyes darted nervously back and forth. Behind him and to either side, the spectators drew nervously away. He sensed their movement, glanced frantically over his shoulder. When he jerked his head back around his face was twisted with desperation. He was all alone.

"No place to run," Stark said grimly. "Time to pack it in."

Burke spat a strangled oath. Snake fast, his hand darted under his coat, popping out with a short-barreled revolver. He was fast, as fast as he'd once hinted, harking back to his days as a gunslinger in Texas.

Stark used the snapping draw, because it was best for the man and the circumstance. His hand and wrist flipped the .45 from its holster, and it bucked and roared in his fist. Burke rocked backward, then turned in a slow pivot. Stark fancied Burke gave him one last hating, disbelieving look as he crumpled to the floor.

"Always figured you for a hideout gun," Stark said tonelessly.

There was a rush of feet, and Prudence was suddenly at his side. "Jim!" she gasped. Her outstretched hands froze inches from him, then dropped to grip his left hand and fold his fingers tightly around the badge still held in his palm. She stared up at him, and in that instant he thought she'd never looked more lovely.

"Thank God you're all right," she said reverently.

"Yeah." Stark's tone was hoarse. He repeated the word. "Yeah."

"Quite a stunt, Jim," U.S. Marshal Evett Nix commented as he came shouldering through the excited spectators. A handful of his deputies were behind him.

"What kind of stunt?" Prudence queried blankly.

Nix grinned. "He lured Burke into sending his henchmen to make a play for him, then brought one of them in alive to testify, so a warrant could be issued for Burke." Nix glanced about at the fallen bodies. "You didn't leave much work for us, Jim."

"Thanks for letting me serve the warrant," Stark said. "I enjoyed it." He handed the badge to Nix. "By the way, I resign."

Prudence looked from one of them to the other in bemusement. "Why did he deputize you?" she asked.

Stark grinned. It hurt his face. "That's easy," he answered. "Tangling with a man like Burke can make enemies of powerful political folks back East, which a man in Evett's position can ill afford to have. When I asked him for a badge, he was happy to oblige. That way, if the arrest blew up in our faces, he could blame a rogue deputy, namely me. But since Burke's pulling iron on me pretty well vindicates the warrant, Evett's free now to take the credit."

Prudence spared Nix one scathing look that made even him wince, then put her attention back on Stark. "What did he mean that you lured Burke into setting a trap for you?"

"You said yourself that he wouldn't risk letting one of his hired thugs get arrested unless he was desperate. Well, after this morning's hearing, I figured Burke was desperate. I let myself be seen, and then made it easy if he wanted to send some boys after me. Turned out that he did."

"So you used yourself as bait?" Prudence demanded with growing outrage.

"Yep." Like the pretty blond bar girl, he'd been the bait, Stark reflected. Except, in his case, he'd also been the trap.

"Jim Stark! Don't you ever do anything that foolish or dangerous again!" Prudence ordered sharply.

Stark stepped closer, until he was looking straight down into her brown eyes, their bodies inches apart. For once, she didn't lift a hand in restraint. "I'm not your personal property, Prudence McKay," Stark drawled.

Chapter Seventeen

"So, Mr. Stark, it is your expert opinion that my client could not have fired the shot that killed the decedent," Prudence summarized succinctly.

"That's correct."

"Thank you, Mr. Stark." Prudence was very brisk and businesslike, but Stark still fancied he caught the faintest flicker of an eyelid in his direction before she looked to the bench. "I have no further questions, Your Honor."

Judge Edward B. Green acknowledged her closing with a nod. "Your witness, Mr. Prosecutor."

Waspish and irritable, Damon Rasters rose, stalked over, and, ignoring the podium, positioned himself directly in front of Stark on the witness stand.

Things had not been going well for the prosecution, if Stark was any judge. Prudence's client came across like the cowhand he was, and certainly not like a cold-blooded sharpshooter. The jury had stirred noticeably when Stark had been called. The notoriety from the brawl with Chin and the shootout with Burke hadn't yet died down.

Stark noted that Ronnie Hall had slipped into the ranks of the spectators and was following the goings-on with his usual eager interest. He and Mindy had delayed their departure in order for the mustanger to clear up some of the legal matters for himself and the other ranchers that had resulted from Burke's death while he was still a defendant in their lawsuit.

"Mr. Stark," Rasters began in rasping tones, "it is true, isn't it, that you make your living by hiring out your services as a mercenary to the highest bidder?"

"I work as a troubleshooter and investigator on cases of my choice," Stark answered levelly. "Price isn't always the determining factor. For example, I recently did some work as a deputy of U.S. Marshal Evett Nix. In other words, I was working for the government just like you do. Except you get a salary. I did my work pro bono. That means without a fee."

"I'm well aware of what it means," Rasters said hotly. Somebody among the spectators stifled a snort of laughter. Stark saw the prosecutor's ears slowly turn a fiery red.

"Would you consider yourself a hired gun, Mr. Stark?"

"I've been called that," Stark said, straight-faced. He resisted the urge to cut a glance at Prudence.

"In other words, your services, including the use of your gun, and even your testimony here today, are available for a fee."

"There are some things I won't do for money," Stark replied laconically. "I won't rob widows and orphans; I won't lie under oath; and, in your shoes, I wouldn't prosecute an innocent man."

Rasters glared. His narrow lips drew into an even thinner line. "You've stated that the suspect couldn't have fired the fatal shot," he tried once again.

"Not from where it was fired," Stark confirmed flatly.

Rasters cocked his head like a fighting rooster. "Are you saying such a shot is impossible?" he demanded triumphantly.

Stark shook his head. "No," he admitted. "I might make it if I knew the gun, and I got lucky. But you couldn't. And neither could Miss McKay's client. He's no trick-shot artist, for crying out loud, he's a cowpuncher." Stark paused to draw breath. "Look, Rasters, you need to be searching for a man with a rifle."

The advice caught Rasters off guard. "What?"

"I'm up here as an expert witness. Maybe you'll listen to what I have to say. The Remington 1875 Army Revolver your suspect carries fires a .44-.40 round. The fact that he was packing it in the area where the bushwhacking took place doesn't make him guilty. An accurate one-hundred-fifty-yard shot with that gun is well-nigh impossible. But it could be made with a rifle, and there are plenty of those around that also fire a .44-.40 round. You ought be looking for an hombre who packs a Winchester 1873 Lever Action, or maybe a Marlin 1888 Repeater in .44-.40 caliber." Stark broke off with a prodding grin. "If you want to hire me, I'd be happy to handle the investigation for you."

It took just half an hour for the jury to find the suspect not guilty.

Ronnie caught up with Stark and Prudence in the hallway outside the courtroom. "Congratulations!"

He clasped Prudence's hand briefly, then pumped Stark's enthusiastically. "I just wanted to say so long. Our train leaves in an hour. Mindy sends her best. She said to remind you about the wedding date."

"We'll be there," Prudence assured him.

Ronnie grinned widely. "That was quite a show in there just now. You had that prosecutor to where he didn't know 'come here' from 'sic 'em!' " He shook his head in wonder. "First, the two of you put Burke out of business, and then you get that fellow cleared of murder charges. You make quite a team." He broke off abruptly as a speculative gleam came into his eye. "Say, maybe you should consider becoming partners and going into business together!"

Stark and Prudence gaped at him. "I work alone," they both said at precisely the same moment.

Ronnie looked back and forth between them; then he started to laugh.